Missing

Becky Citra

ORCA BOOK PUBLISHERS

Library and Archives Canada Cataloguing in Publication

Citra, Becky
Missing / Becky Citra.

Issued also in electronic format.
ISBN 978-1-55469-345-0

I. Title.
PS8555.I87M58 2011   jc813'.54   C2010-907946-9

First published in the United States, 2011
Library of Congress Control Number: 2010941924

Summary: When Thea's father gets a job at a guest ranch in the Cariboo, Thea earns
the trust of an abused horse, solves an old mystery and makes a new friend.

*Orca Book Publishers is dedicated to preserving the environment and has
printed this book on Forest Stewardship Council® certified paper.*

Orca Book Publishers gratefully acknowledges the support for its publishing
programs provided by the following agencies: the Government of Canada through the
Canada Book Fund and the Canada Council for the Arts, and the Province of British
Columbia through the BC Arts Council and the Book Publishing Tax Credit.

Cover design by Teresa Bubela
Cover photography by Getty Images

ORCA BOOK PUBLISHERS
PO Box 5626, Stn. B
Victoria, BC Canada
V8R 6S4

ORCA BOOK PUBLISHERS
PO Box 468
CUSTER, WA USA
98240-0468

www.orcabook.com
Printed and bound in Canada.

16 15 14 13 • 6 5 4 3

For my brother John

One

It's nearly the end of June, and I'm at the café, sitting in my usual booth at the back. I must look like the biggest loser. Nowhere to go after school but the café, where I work on homework. Not that there's anyone to see me. No one that matters anyway.

"How's the homework going?" says Dad. He's wiping the table in the booth next to mine, scrubbing at a particularly stubborn ketchup blob. Usually he's behind the grill, frying burgers and eggs, but the waitress has gone home early with a headache. Dad's boss, Sid, took over the grill and sent Dad out here. The café is mostly empty; there's just a woman and a small child eating ice cream at the window table.

Dad lingers to chat. "Want a Coke?"

"No thanks."

"School go okay today?"

"Great," I lie.

I don't fool Dad. "Give it a chance," he says. "You can't expect to have a lot of friends instantly."

I bend over my book so I don't have to lie anymore. Dad doesn't know what he's talking about. It takes time to make friends, and that's what I don't have. Sid's regular cook will be back next week and then Dad will be officially out of work. Again. He's been scanning the newspaper for jobs for weeks and leaving resumes around town, but there's nothing here. We'll be moving again.

And since when does Dad care anyway?

The page of math problems blurs over, and I blink hard. I've been like this all day. Fragile.

"Hey, Dusty, get in here," calls Sid. Dad's jaw tightens for a moment. I guess he isn't having the best day either. He takes his time going back to the kitchen, and I concentrate on the next math problem.

Now I really feel like crying. I have a whole page of these stupid problems to do. I think longingly of the novel that I borrowed from the school library. *The Horse Whisperer.* I've seen the movie three times, but I've never read the book. For some reason, I didn't know there was a book, and it was the best moment of my week when I spotted it in the trolley of books waiting to be shelved.

It's fat, and I figure I should really save it for school. It would fill up a lot of empty lunch hours.

I turn back to my math book. Who makes up these problems? What do they have to do with real life? An hour later I've done as much as I can, which is a little less than half. I'm already behind in all my subjects, and my worst nightmare is that I fail grade eight and have to do it all over again. I've always thought of myself as an average student, but this school is way harder than the last one.

When we lived in the Fraser Valley, I went to the same school from kindergarten to grade four. I liked it a lot, and I had three best friends. After all the bad stuff happened, Dad didn't want anything to do with our old life. We came north and started moving from small town to small town in the Cariboo. That's when things got even worse. None of Dad's jobs last, and I want to go back to our old life, but I know Dad never will. I still miss my friends, though they've probably forgotten all about me, and I miss the Valley.

The café is empty now, except for Sid, Dad and me. Dad slides onto the seat opposite me with a mug of coffee. His face looks gray. Sid gives him ten-minute breaks and if Dad takes even one gazillionth of a second longer, Sid starts griping about how the café isn't made of money. It's the end of the night, so it's Dad's last break. Then he'll clean up the kitchen and we can go home.

The door opens and a man comes in. He's a big man with a red face, wearing jeans and boots that look brand-new, and a cowboy hat that doesn't fit his head quite right. Dad has his back to him and he doesn't turn around. A customer at this time of night means the café will be late closing. Sid doesn't ever turn down the chance to make some money.

But Sid wants to go home too—the air-conditioning is on the fritz and there are two half circles of sweat under his armpits. "Sorry, we're closing," he says.

The man smiles and says, "I'm not here for a meal. I'm just spreading the word around town that I'm looking to hire someone out at my ranch. You must get a lot of people in and out of here during the day. Know anyone who's looking for work?"

Dad's listening now, I can tell, even though he's pretending to drink his coffee. As for me, I want to scream, "Yes! Over here!" I can't believe this. Some guy just wanders in here with a job tucked in his pocket. I don't even care what the job is. I'm sure Dad can do it. Maybe, just maybe, we can stay in one town for more than a few months.

Sid nods his head our way and says, "You might want to talk to Dusty."

The man hesitates for a second and then approaches our table. He reaches out his hand and says in a loud voice, "Stan Tulworth. Everyone calls me Tully."

Dad says, "Dusty Taylor." He shakes hands and then adds, "And this is my daughter, Thea."

"Thea. What a charming name. Short for Theadora?"

I nod, slightly embarrassed. Most people have never heard of the name Theadora. I'm hoping Tully will say more about the job. I'm trying to stay cool inside, but I can hear my heart thumping. I'm feeling so hopeful, but I should know better by now.

"Pleased to meet you both," says Tully. "Can you give me a few minutes of your time?"

Dad shrugs and Tully, taking that for a yes, slides his bulk into the seat beside me. He spreads his hands on the table. He's wearing a large silver ring with a chunky black stone. "I bought the Double R Ranch," he says without any preamble.

"Is that so?" says Dad.

"So you've heard of the place?" Tully asks.

Dad shakes his head. "Sorry. We're fairly new in town ourselves."

Tully exhales loudly. "It's a big spread up on Gumboot Lake, about twenty kilometers out of town. A guest ranch. There's ten cabins along the lakeshore and a lodge. Last owner got rid of the horses and closed it up about three years ago. Put a caretaker in there while he kept it on the market." Tully beams. "Then I bought it. In April."

Dad takes a sip of his coffee.

"Thing is," says Tully, "I'm planning to bring the guests back and breed quarter horses as well. High-quality horses."

"You run a ranch before?" says Dad.

"No," says Tully. "But I like a challenge."

"Ah," says Dad.

"The horses will have to wait until next summer," says Tully. "This year I'm focusing on fixing the place up. Most of the cabins are pretty run-down. I'm looking for someone with some carpentry skills. I want to gut at least three of the cabins and fix them up real nice."

I don't tend to think of Dad and me as lucky. But this is our lucky night. Dad is really good at building stuff, and he likes it way better than cooking hamburgers. My breath comes out in a whoosh. "Dad built a whole house once," I say. It's true. It took eight months and it was the longest I had stayed in one school since I was nine.

"Is that so?" says Tully.

But Dad says, "I don't know."

I know right away what he's thinking. It's the talk about horses. Ever since Mom's accident four years ago, Dad can't even stand to think about horses. I don't get how Dad can wipe out a whole part of our lives, but he has. He changes the subject if I even mention horses. A lump fills my throat.

Tully is waiting and Dad says, "I don't know," again.

Tully takes a wallet out of his back pocket, opens it and slides out a business card. He lays it on the table. "Here's my card. I'll be around the ranch all next weekend. Come on out and we can talk."

Tully stands up, shakes hands with Dad again, and then he's gone. Tully doesn't know Dad from a hole in the wall, but he has more or less just offered him a job. I'm trying to figure out what this means. If I were religious, maybe I'd think Tully was some kind of guardian angel. But I'm not, so I don't know what to think.

Dad goes back into the kitchen and leaves the card lying on the table, right where Tully dropped it. I study it for a minute. The words *Double R Guest Ranch* and Tully's name, phone number and email address are printed in black letters above a photograph of a horse galloping across a green field.

The stupid lump fills my throat again. I pick up the card and slip it into the plastic sleeve inside my binder.

Two

It's Friday and I've been waiting all week for Dad to tell me if we're going to see Tully about the job. Dad's supposed to work on Saturday and Sunday (his last two days of work), but just until five. I figure there'll be plenty of time to drive out to the ranch before it gets dark.

I'm in the school library, reading *The Horse Whisperer*. I can't put it down—it's that great—and for the first time since I came to this school I wish the lunch hours were longer than forty-five minutes.

I'm sitting in the back corner of the library, far away from the row of windows that faces out into the hallway. I don't want people to see me and think that I don't have anyone to hang out with. I've been going to this school for two months now, and lunch hours are definitely the hardest.

I can fake it during class time. Open my book and recopy notes or work on homework. Anything to look busy. But at lunchtime everyone spills into the hallways. Lots of kids head downtown for junk food. I wish I had someone to go with. But not one person ever speaks to me. Not one. It's like I'm invisible or something. Or maybe someone stuck one of those paper signs—*Kick Me* or *Contagious* or *No Trespassing*—on my back on the first day for a joke and I didn't know it.

I'm pretty good at observing other people, and within a few weeks of being at this school I had the groups figured out. It's not like it's a very big school. You start to recognize faces. There's the popular group of course, and I've identified most of the kids in that. They're the noisiest in the hallway. Confident. Happy. Then there are the kids who stand outside the school grounds every lunch hour, smoking. And of course, the jocks, who make all the school teams. And finally there are kids just banding together for survival. It's pretty much the same as my last school. Same groups, different faces.

Well, that's not exactly true. This school has a group I've never encountered before. I walked past them the other day just before school started.

About a dozen kids were standing in a circle holding hands. I tried not to stare, but I did catch the eye of one boy. He smiled at me and I looked away. But I was eaten up by curiosity. What were they doing? Then a bunch of the smokers walked by, and one of them yelled out something like, "Hey, God, I've been saaaaaved," and then I got it. They're some kind of religious group.

The bell rings and I close my book with a sigh. English, a double block of science, and then freedom.

⊱

Dad's truck won't start, and I panic, thinking that everything is going to be wrecked after all. I had finally persuaded Dad to at least talk to Tully. Dad hung up his apron for the last time today at exactly five o'clock, and we went to one of the nicest restaurants in town for a celebration dinner. I worried that we were spending too much money (Dad doesn't *have* the job yet), but Dad was in a good mood and told me to order whatever I wanted. I don't think I really realized until then how much he had hated working for Sid. I figured this splurge of a dinner was a promising sign and decided to enjoy my lasagna and double-fudge-brownie sundae without feeling guilty.

And now the stupid truck won't start and it's almost seven o'clock. Dad's bent over the open hood, fiddling with something. Worry eats at me like ants on a saucer of jam. Tully must have decided by now that we aren't coming. What if he gives the job to someone else? How many other guys in town did he talk to? What if, right at this very minute, some other guy with a stupid degree in carpentry is driving up the road to the Double R Ranch?

"Jump in the truck and try starting it again, Thea," says Dad. I climb in and turn the key. I can actually feel sweat trickle down my back. The engine roars to life. Dad slams the hood down, and I slide over to my side of the seat as he scrambles in.

We don't talk on the way to the ranch. Dad's tired and I'm too anxious about what's going to happen. About ten kilometers out of town we turn onto a gravel road. Our truck has no suspension left, so it feels like we're bouncing from pothole to pothole. I stare out the side window, watching trees and fields and the occasional house slide by. In one field, three horses are cantering up a slope, and I keep them in sight as long as I can.

Fifteen minutes later we turn under a big log archway that has the words *Double R Guest Ranch* burned into the wood. I see the lake first, a smooth plate of emerald green water, and then a huge log house half hidden in a grove of pine trees.

Dad pulls up near the house and stops the truck. Tully is standing on the porch of the house as if he's been waiting for us. He's still wearing his new jeans and boots, but he's taken off the cowboy hat and you can see a tan line across his forehead. He has curly gray hair that springs all over the place.

Three dogs race in front of him, barking, as he strides over to the truck. He is all smiles while we climb out. "You made it," he says. "You'll have to say hello to my boys first, or they won't give you any peace."

He makes the introductions. The long-legged black dog with a laughing mouth is Max, the brown and white springer spaniel is Bob and the little gray terrier is Tinker. Max and Tinker crowd around our legs, tails wagging, and Bob hangs back a little. "Hush now, that's enough barking," says Tully. "They're all strays from the SPCA, and they get along splendidly. Bob is a little shy, but he'll come around."

I've fallen in love with them already, but I think Bob is my favorite. He has long floppy ears, and eyes like melted chocolate. I reach out my hand and he approaches cautiously and sniffs my fingers.

"I'll give you a tour and then we'll go inside and talk," says Tully.

He takes us for a walk along a dirt road that follows the shore of the lake. The dogs come with us, galloping into the bushes and chasing after scents. The road winds through pine trees, and the ground is covered by a soft blanket of dusty needles. Scattered along the road on the lakeside are log cabins, all different sizes, each one tucked into the trees and with its own narrow wooden dock. Tully points out which cabins are in pretty good shape and which ones he wants to renovate. I'm not really listening. A breeze wafts off the water; for the first time today I feel cool.

At one of the larger cabins we walk out onto the dock and look at the glassy lake. The sun is hovering over the top of the hill on the opposite shore, and the water has turned from emerald green to a pale copper. It's so beautiful it makes me catch my breath.

"Gumboot Lake is two kilometers long and half a kilometer wide," says Tully. "There are a few summer places at the other end and a couple of year-round homes. This end of the lake stays pretty quiet."

The road becomes narrower, with bushes crowding both sides. Tully says there isn't much more to see, just one cabin that's so far gone it's not worth fixing up. We head back. I trail a little behind, trying to imagine what this place must have been like when it was full of guests and there were horses.

Ahead of me, Tully is doing a lot of talking, and Dad nods his head a few times. When we get back near the lodge, Tully points out a barn and corrals and a few other outbuildings. The barn is made of logs too and has a tin roof. Behind it a huge field slopes up toward a ridge of forest.

While we're standing there, the sun disappears behind the hill. The lake loses its magic. The water is black and the opposite shore is a dark smudge. I shiver slightly.

"Coffee time," says Tully. "Come on inside."

We walk up four steps onto a wide porch that wraps around the whole building. Wooden lawn chairs with faded striped cushions are scattered along it, facing the lake. It looks like an inviting place to curl up with a book.

I come to a dead stop when we go through the door. We're in a huge open room with wood floors and bright rugs, an enormous stone fireplace and lots of overstuffed leather armchairs and couches. The kitchen is at one end, with a big island and a mass of gleaming copper pans hanging from a round rack suspended from the high ceiling. There's one gigantic table that would seat twenty people. A balcony runs all around the room and I figure there must be lots of rooms upstairs.

The room is amazing, but that's not what stops me in my tracks. It's the framed photographs on every wall. I'm not lying when I say there must be hundreds.

"Impressive," says Dad behind me. "Who's the photographer?"

"I am," says Tully, and I can hear the pride in his voice. "Take a look, if you like."

Tully sets out a pot of coffee, mugs, hot chocolate for me and a plate of cookies on one end of the long table. Dad and I wander about the room. The photographs are beautiful. Buildings, people, animals and scenery. The colors are rich and vibrant. Some of the places I recognize, like the Great Pyramids in Egypt and the Eiffel Tower. But I have no idea where most of the photographs were taken.

"You've traveled a lot," says Dad.

"All around the world," says Tully.

"Even to Africa," I say. I'm standing in front of a wall of photographs of African animals: cheetahs, elephants, leopards and giraffes, and some that I can't identify. The animals are so clear that they look like they could step right out of their frames. I can see the individual hairs in a lion's mane.

"I went on a safari last fall," says Tully. "To the Masai Mara in Kenya. A truly spectacular place."

"Wow," I say. "I'd love to do that."

I figure you could spend hours in this room, looking at photographs and not getting bored. I also figure Tully must have lots of awesome stories about his travels.

Tully pours the coffee, and he and Dad sit down at the table. I take my mug of hot chocolate and a cookie and go back to the African pictures. I'm close enough to hear everything Dad and Tully say.

Tully gets right to the point. "I need someone to work on the cabins until the snow comes," he says.

I hold my breath.

"That could work out," says Dad slowly.

"You and Thea can stay out here rent-free, if you want," says Tully casually. "Cabin three is in pretty good shape. Just needs a bit of sweeping out. That way you don't have to drive out from town every day. And Thea could take the school bus for the last couple of weeks of school."

"I don't know about that," says Dad. "I'd want to pay some rent."

Tully shrugs. "I'm sure we could agree on something."

I turn the idea over in my head while I go eye to eye with a leopard. Staying here would be better, way better, than staying in the boiling hot trailer all summer. I think about swimming in the lake and reading in one of those lawn chairs with the striped cushions.

"I think we should do it," I pipe up.

"I have ulterior motives," says Tully with a laugh. "I could do with some company. And I need to test out some of my guest-ranch cooking."

"Meals on top of the salary?" says Dad.

"I don't like eating alone," says Tully simply. "And it's no more work to cook for three than for one."

"I don't want to impose," says Dad. He sounds a little tense, like this is all happening too fast.

"Then how about you look after your own breakfast and lunch and I'll cook dinner?"

Tully's talking like it's all decided, that we're going to take him up on his offer. For a few seconds I think that maybe it's a little odd that he would do all this for two strangers. Then I push that thought away. Tully needs the help. Dad needs the work. It's that simple.

"That's a great idea," I say. "I hate cooking."

Tully laughs, and then Dad laughs too.

"Okay," says Dad. He shakes Tully's hand. "Deal."

Tully's drawn up some rough sketches of what he wants to do in the cabins he's renovating, and he spreads them out on the table. There's a scratch at the door and a sharp bark. Tully gets up and opens the door, and the dogs bound inside. Max and Bob flop down on the floor, panting. Tinker goes over to a big water dish in the kitchen and slurps noisily. Tully and Dad start talking about beams and studs and two-by-fours.

I take another cookie and drift outside. I want to have a look inside the barn.

❧

The heavy door creaks when I push it open. I'm immediately hit with the smell of hay. An image of another barn slams into my head. Not a clear image, not like one of Tully's photographs. It's actually more of a bombardment of my senses. The pungent odor of horse sweat, the rustle of straw, the rhythmic chewing of hay, the smell of saddle soap and leather. There's a hard choking feeling in my chest, and I take a few big breaths to steady myself.

It's four years since I've been in a horse barn. Four years since Mom died.

In a few seconds, my eyes adjust to the dim light. A cement aisle runs up the middle, with a row of box stalls on either side. I count twelve stalls altogether. I peer into one. Old straw is scattered on the ground, and a black feed bucket rests on its side.

If I close my eyes, I can feel the horses standing like ghosts in the silent stalls. I push open a door and look into a small room filled with horse tack, all jumbled up: saddles stacked on top of each other and leaning against the wall, a tangle of halters and bridles and ropes, some hanging on hooks, some fallen on the ground.

A shroud of dust on everything. Not like that other barn, everything saddle-soaped and in its place, bridles hanging under the name of each horse engraved on a wooden sign. I still remember some of the names. *Dancer, Tippy, Major, Skipper, Magic.* And *Monty.* I will never forget Monty.

Something deep inside me stirs. I could fix this up, clean up the tack. I deflate rapidly. *What for?* Dad shuts right down if I even talk about getting horses again.

There's one more door at the back of the barn, and it leads outside. Behind the barn is a long rectangular corral of hard-packed dirt, weeds growing in the corners. Inside the corral, at one end, there's a small circular pen made of metal rods. At the other end of the corral is a slope-roofed wooden shelter with a bathtub full of water beside it. On the outside of the fence, hay bales are neatly stacked and covered with a blue tarp. A bale has been pulled from the pile and lies on the ground, split into flakes. It's pale green and fresh-smelling. *New.*

My heart thumping, I stare at the shelter. I see just a shadow at first, hidden in the back corner. Then the shadow shifts. A dark eye is watching me, and my heart starts to race even faster. I lean over the corral fence and softly say, "Hey."

Tully said they got rid of all the horses, but for some reason this one must have been left behind.

I can see now that it's a big horse—more than sixteen hands, I bet—black with a white stripe down his face and one white sock on a front foot. A piece of hay hangs from his mouth, but he isn't chewing. He looks wary.

I scan the corral fence and find the gate. I unhook the latch and let myself into the corral, closing the gate carefully behind me. The horse keeps watching me. I can see the whites of his eyes now.

"Hey," I say again. I approach slowly and extend my hand.

Nothing prepares me for the explosion of sound and movement. The horse bolts from the shelter, kicking out at the thin wooden wall with a cracking sound. I jump back but his heavy body slams into me and knocks me to the ground. Dust swirls in my eyes. I can't tell where he is, but I can hear him snorting and blowing through his nostrils. In a panic, I pull myself up and stumble to the fence. I manage to climb over and drop to safety on the other side.

I take a few huge breaths. I'm okay, not even a little bit hurt. Just scared. I wipe my dusty hands on my jeans. The horse has galloped across to the far side of the corral, behind the metal pen. He's quiet now, but I can tell he's upset. His sides are heaving and the whites of his eyes still show.

I stay outside the fence, watching the horse for a few minutes. My eyes drift to the round metal pen at the far end of the corral. Something jogs my memory. We had one just like it beside our barn. It's where Mom and Dad used to work with the young horses that came to our stable for training.

I push those thoughts away. Soon it's too dark to see properly, and the horse is swallowed up by the night. I hear his hooves clumping on the hard ground as he moves, shadowlike, back into the safety of his shelter.

As I walk back to the lodge, my head is whirling with possibilities, but I have already decided not to tell Dad about the horse.

Not tonight, when he can still change his mind about staying here.

Three

Tully said Dad can have a job at least until the snow flies. That means I won't have to change schools and be the new kid again until probably November. And by then, *maybe*, with this streak of luck we're having, something else will have turned up and we'll be able to stay.

Dad gives one week's notice on the trailer, and we move out to the ranch the following weekend. Our truck is loaded with boxes of groceries and everything we own, which isn't much. Four years ago, Dad sold everything that reminded him of our old life.

Cabin three is one of the bigger ones, with two large bedrooms, a bathroom, a kitchen and a sitting area. Tully has opened all the windows and swept out several years' accumulation of dust, dirt and pine cones left by squirrels. A fresh breeze blows the curtains, and the lake glitters in the sun.

After we've put everything away in the cupboards and closets, Dad goes up to the lodge to talk to Tully. There's half an hour until dinnertime, so I slip away to the barn, where I go straight to the back corral.

The horse is standing in the shade of his shelter, his nose pressed to the wall. Flies buzz around his ears. I can see a whole lot better in the bright daylight, and I hate what I see. His coat is scruffy, his mane a tangled nest. Several thick corded lines, which look like scars, cross his hocks.

I know better than to go inside the corral this time. I talk to him for a few minutes, hoping he'll turn around. I wish I had something to offer him; next time I'll bring an apple. I stay as long as I can and then whisper, "Goodbye."

He knows I am there, I'm sure of it, but he doesn't even twitch an ear.

⚹

I ask Tully about the horse at dinner. I figure it's safe now. After all, we've taken over the cabin and Dad can hardly change his mind. We're all sitting at one end of the long table, eating ham, scalloped potatoes and peas It's delicious.

Dad doesn't say anything, but his fork pauses over his plate and he stops chewing. I feel nervous and hopeful at the same time. After all, Dad always loved horses. Before.

"So you found Renegade," says Tully. He helps himself to more potatoes. Tully has a huge appetite. He's already devoured more than Dad and me put together.

"Is he yours?" I say. *Renegade,* I think. The name suits him.

"In a manner of speaking," says Tully. "I don't think you can say that Renegade belongs to anyone. But he came with the ranch so I guess that makes him mine."

Dad is still not talking.

I swallow. "There's scars on his legs," I say. "And his coat's a mess."

"I know," says Tully.

"Someone should clean him up," I say. I can't help it; my voice sounds accusatory.

Tully shrugs. "He won't let anyone near him. I throw him some hay and a little grain every day and fill his bathtub with water. That's the best I can do."

There's so much I want to know about Renegade. "Where did he come from?"

"The guy I bought the ranch from picked him up at a horse sale. Said he seemed tame enough.

He figures he was drugged for the sale. He had no idea what kind of trouble he was buying until he got him home. Turns out the horse has never been broke to ride, even though he's eight years old."

"What a waste," I say.

Tully sighs. "I'll have to deal with him one of these days, but right now I feel he's not really hurting anything by being here."

I chew my piece of ham slowly. Ideas turn round and round in my head.

We're not finished dinner yet, but Dad stands up. I hope that he is going to say something about Renegade, but he doesn't. He thanks Tully for the meal and leaves.

Tully and I load the dishwasher together, and then Tully whistles to the dogs, who leap up from under the long table and follow him outside.

At dinner, Tully had told us that he's been cleaning up the small office off the kitchen. He calls it a work in progress and says he only gets to it when the weather is too bad to go outside. There are piles of stuff from back before there were computers: receipts, lined notebooks filled with bookings, bills of sale from horse sales, even a book of old recipes.

Tully says he's chucking out most of the stuff, but he's discovered some boxes of old guest books that he says are keepers. He's been reading through them, trying to get a flavor of what the ranch was like in its prime. He says it's amazing how far away guests came from: Australia, France, Germany.

He's cleared off a shelf in the main room under the windows and he plans to arrange the guest books there in order of their year. The books are spread all over the floor in front of the shelf now. There must be fifteen or twenty of them. I've got nothing else to do, so I take over the job, sorting through the books to see which one comes first.

Some of them have the year on the spine but for most I have to look inside. The oldest books have black-and-white photographs of the guests. Then there are some with color photographs, but the newest books have no photographs at all, just written comments.

There are huge gaps in the dates, and I remember Tully saying that the ranch wasn't always run as a guest ranch. I can't find any books between 1965 and 1985 or between 1998 and 2004. When I'm finished organizing the books on the shelf, I take out the oldest book—dated 1953—and plop down in a leather armchair to look at it. It has a worn brown leather cover. The paper is yellowed and the writing faded, The pages are divided in half; on one side are the comments from the guests and on the other side are slightly blurry black-and-white photographs. Most of the photographic were taken in front of the lodge. Families lined up in a row, parents' hands around their children's shoulders, everyone smiling stiffly into the camera.

The date on the first page is June 7, 1953. I turn pages, studying the faces that stare out at me, deciphering the handwriting. Some of the writing is tight and cramped, some sprawling, some with big rounded letters. After a while the comments all start to sound the same: *fantastic place...a bit of paradise... terrific food...we'll be back.*

On one page someone—probably a child— has printed *Don't forget to give Benny a carrot every day from me.* I look at the photograph of a man, a woman and a little girl who looks about nine. She has braids and a wide smile with a gap between her front teeth. I imagine her falling in love with some kind old horse who probably carried her around the ranch for a week.

I wonder if our family ever looked like that, like we really belonged together. Mom wasn't living with us when she died, so maybe we never were much of a family. When Mom left, I didn't get it. I kept asking Dad where she was and when she was coming back.

I finally found out the truth when Samantha Higgens, a girl in my grade-four class, told me. She'd heard her mother and father talking about it. She said Mom had moved in with a trainer that she and Dad had known for years. According to Samantha, she wasn't planning on living with us ever again. End of story. That's what she said. *End of story.*

Only it wasn't the end of the story. And how would Samantha know anyway? Before I had time to find out if Mom was ever coming back, her horse rolled over on top of her on a slippery hillside and she was killed. She was riding by herself on Sumas Mountain on a colt that had just been broken. A search party found her late at night. I remember the phone waking me up and Dad coming in and sitting on the end of my bed and telling me.

Thinking about Mom and my old life makes me feel crappy. I push it out of my mind now and turn to the next page in the guest book: *July 10, 1953.* Tucked into the book's spine is a piece of tightly folded yellowed newspaper. Curious, I spread it out, smoothing the creases. It's a clipping that someone has cut out carefully with scissors. The date at the top says *July 9, 1954*, almost exactly one year later than the date in the book.

I read the article slowly.

DOUBLE TRAGEDY AT
CARIBOO GUEST RANCH

On the afternoon of July 7, four-year-old Livia Willard was reported missing from the Double R Guest Ranch in the heart of British Columbia's Cariboo. Wayne and Joan Willard from North Vancouver and their three daughters, fourteen-year-old Esta, eight-year-old Iris and four-year-old Livia, had arrived on Saturday, July 2, at the guest ranch for their annual holiday. They were accompanied by twenty-six-year old Melissa Ryerson, the Willards' niece, who has been visiting the family from England since early May.

Livia was reported missing at three o'clock. Her parents had returned to Vancouver the day before due to a family emergency, leaving their daughters in the care of their niece. They planned to return to the ranch later in the week. The Willards were notified immediately of their daughter's disappearance and left Vancouver in the late afternoon to drive back to the ranch. Their vehicle was struck by a truck on the Trans-Canada Highway near the small town of Boston Bar. Both parents were pronounced dead on arrival at the hospital in Hope.

At the present moment, the Willard girls, Esta and Iris, and Melissa Ryerson are under the care of Pat and Margaret Hunter, owners of the Double R Guest Ranch, until Melissa's mother, Jane Ryerson, arrives from England. She is expected early tomorrow morning.

Livia Willard was last seen wearing pink shorts, a pink T-shirt and running shoes with bunnies on them. She is blond and blue-eyed. A massive search is continuing for the little girl, and the police say that at this time they have no leads. Ranch owner Pat Hunter has declined to comment.

There are two photographs on this page in the guest book: one of a young grinning couple and one of a family—a man, a woman and three girls. In the comment section beside the family picture, someone has written neatly *We had a wonderful time as usual. See you next year! Joan and Wayne Willard.* Underneath are the three girls' names: *Esta* in perfectly formed slanting letters, *Iris* in slightly uneven loopy handwriting and *Livia* in large babyish printing.

I check the names of the girls in the newspaper article again to figure out who is who and then study the photograph. That must be Esta at the edge of the picture, a little apart from everyone else. She would have been thirteen then, like me, because the photograph was taken a year before the newspaper article. She's tall, almost as tall as her mother, and she has dark hair and eyes. She's frowning and looks like she'd rather be anywhere than posing for this photograph. Iris is standing in front of her mother. She has straight shoulder-length hair and a thin face with a pointed chin. She's smiling, but her smile looks self-conscious.

Livia is beautiful. She has a mass of blond curls, a heart-shaped face and huge eyes. She is standing beside her father, holding his hand. A stuffed bear dangles from her other hand.

See you next year. I imagine Joan Willard writing that in the guest book, the girls waiting their turn to sign their names, the parents bursting with pride that Livia could print her name at three years old. The owners of the ranch must have gathered everyone together for their photograph, like they did with every visitor. Then the Willards would have piled into their car and headed back to Vancouver. For some reason I even imagine that the car was one of those old-fashioned station wagons with the wood trim.

See you next year.

According to the newspaper article, they *had* come back. But there wouldn't be anything in the guest book that year. No enthusiastic *We had a wonderful time.*

I flip through the rest of the book to see if there are any more newspaper articles, but I don't find anything. I don't know how long that piece of newspaper has been hidden in the book but I feel that it is important to put it back.

I fold it carefully and then take one last look at Livia's face before I close the book. A tiny shiver runs up my back. Children don't go missing forever, do they? I wonder where they found her.

Four

The next day at school I have a free block last period so I go to the computer lab and google *Livia Willard.* Nothing comes up. I guess the story isn't important enough, but I'm dying to know what happened to her. I type in *Double R Guest Ranch.* Tully has set up a website with some photos of the lake and cabins. I get a few other hits too, mostly tourism sites with directions, maps and some old guest reviews. No mention of a little girl disappearing almost sixty years ago.

Before the bell rings at the end of the school day, I type in *horse training + round pen* and am amazed at how much information there is. We're supposed to have permission from a teacher to use the printer, but there's no one around, so I print off six articles.

My cell phone vibrates. It's Dad. Something's come up and he can't come to town to pick me up. I have to take the school bus. I have a note for the driver, asking him to drop me off at the ranch gate, but I didn't think I would have to use it until tomorrow. The bell rings and I start worrying about how I'm going to find the right bus and who I'll have to sit with. I turn off the computer and join the crowds of kids waiting outside the school.

When three buses finally pull up to the curb, I have no idea which one is mine. I hang back for a bit, trying to figure out what to do. I see a girl who's in my PE class and who was my partner once for badminton. She was pretty nice, so I ask her if she knows which bus goes out to Gumboot Lake. She points to the last bus, and I fall in at the tail end of the line of kids pushing their way on.

There's an empty seat right behind the bus driver. I give him my note, and he grunts that the closest he can let me off is Thurston Road. I haven't a clue where that is, but I nod and slide into the seat. At least I don't have to walk down the aisle with everyone staring at me. I gaze out the window, shutting out the noise, and watch the scenery slide by. The bus turns off the highway onto the gravel road. It makes lots of stops and gradually empties until it's absolutely quiet, and I'm thinking I'm the only one left. I don't want to turn around and look though.

Then someone flops into the seat behind me and a voice says, "Hi. You're Thea, aren't you?"

I don't have much choice, so I turn around. It's a boy from my social studies class, perched on the edge of the seat. I know him from somewhere else too, but I can't think where. He has fairly long blond hair and he's tanned and wearing a baseball cap. I even know his name—Van—though I'm shocked that he knows mine.

"That's right," I say.

"I'm Van," he says.

"I know," I say, and then my cheeks turn hot. "I heard your name in social studies," I mumble.

"I thought you lived in town," he says.

"I did. We just moved out to the Double R Guest Ranch. My dad's working for the owner."

"You're getting off at my stop then." He grins. "You'll have to. That's where the bus turns around."

I feel awkward, twisted around in my seat to face him, and I'm not sure what to do next. He stands up. "It's just around the corner."

Van gets off the bus first, and I follow him. I know where I am now. On the left side of the road there's a big field with a brown shed at one end, and on the other side is thick forest. Thurston Road goes off to the right. The ranch is about a quarter of a kilometer from here.

The bus turns around and rumbles away in a cloud of dust. Van jumps into the bushes and comes out a few seconds later, lifting a blue bike over the ditch. It's kind of battered-looking and has a bent fender. I guess he doesn't worry about it being stolen.

"I keep it stashed here," he says. "I live at the end of the lake."

I remember Tully telling us that there are some year-round homes farther down the lake. That makes Van sort of a neighbor.

He walks beside me, pushing the bike.

"You don't have to walk with me," I say.

"I like walking," says Van.

He leans over, picks up a rock and skitters it down the road in front of us. "How do you like our school?" he says.

So he knows that I'm new; that means he must have noticed me, but that's all it means. It's not a big school, and new people stick out like sore thumbs.

I shrug and say, "It's just a school."

Van doesn't say anything after that and I'm furious at myself. I should have at least said it's all right. When we get to the ranch gate, he says, "See you," and hops on his bike and pedals off fast.

I try to think where I've seen him before, but I can't place him.

After I get home, I go for a swim off the end of the dock in front of our cabin. The water is warm on the surface but icy cold where my feet dangle down. I have to swim through a patch of lily pads to get out to where it's clear. I duck right under, letting my long hair float around me, and then push it out of my eyes when I pop to the surface. I feel the sweat washing off me. I float on my back for a few minutes, staring at the blue sky, and then swim back to the dock.

A breeze has come up, ruffling the lake. I lie face-down on the smooth weathered boards, the hot sun soaking into my back. The water laps gently under the dock, making it rock. I can hear hammering in the distance: Dad working on cabin five. It's peaceful and a hundred times better than living in that crummy trailer.

When I'm dry, I go inside and change into shorts and a halter top. I've got homework, but that can wait until tonight. I grab an apple for Renegade, cut it into four pieces and head out to the barn.

Renegade's standing in the middle of the corral, his head drooping, his tail gently swishing away flies.

He lifts his head when he sees me; his dark eyes look suspicious. I climb onto the top rail and hold out a piece of apple for him. I make a clicking sound with my tongue, encouraging him to walk over and take a look. "I won't touch you," I say.

He doesn't move. His gaze shifts away from me, outside the corral to the big field that slopes up to the ridge of forest and the hills in the distance. His ears are pricked forward. I try to see what he's looking at, but there's nothing there. And then I spot two tawny deer bounding through the long grass. I have a feeling nothing gets past Renegade.

"I bet you'd like to be out there too," I say. "I bet you'd like to gallop across that field instead of being cooped up in here." For a second I think about opening the gate and letting him out. I ditch that idea quickly. He'd probably never come back and I'd be in major trouble.

I fed Renegade this morning before school—hay and some oats that I found in a metal drum in the barn. Tully says he's happy to hand over that job to me. I fill up the bathtub now with a hose that stretches from the barn and retrieve the empty grain bucket, which Renegade has kicked against the fence. As I go in and out of the corral, I keep my eye on him, but he is disinterested, still staring at the distant hills. I toss another flake of hay over the fence, drop the apples on top and wait.

I like the way Renegade smells. I like the smell of the hay, and I even like the smell of the manure stomped into the dusty ground.

I wait a little longer.

My eyes flick to the round pen at the end of the corral. Somehow I know that it's the key to working with Renegade. If only I knew how to use it. Tonight I'm planning to read the stuff I got off the Internet.

At last Renegade drifts over to the bathtub and drinks, raising his head nervously every few seconds. Water streams from his muzzle. He stretches out his neck and nudges at a piece of apple. His lips close on it and he chews.

He is close now, so close. Only the fence is between us. I hold my breath. I could reach out and touch him. But I don't.

❧

Tully has a surprise at dinner. "We have our first guest," he says.

"I thought you weren't opening until next summer," I say.

Tully has barbecued us each a steak and baked some potatoes, and we're eating on the porch. Dad jumped in the lake to clean himself up after he finished working.

His hair is still wet and slicked back, and he looks more relaxed than I've seen him for a long time.

"I'm not," says Tully. "But this is one determined lady."

It turns out he's been emailing back and forth all day with some woman in England. Tully says her name is Marion Wilson and she has friends who stayed here ten years ago and highly recommended it.

"When is she coming?" I say.

"Next week," says Tully. "I told her we weren't set up for riding or anything. She says she just wants to relax. She doesn't eat breakfast, wants a bag lunch and will have dinner with us. She sounds like a very nice lady."

"What cabin are you going to put her in?" says Dad.

"I think cabin two, next to you guys."

"How long will she stay?" I ask.

"She wasn't sure. She wants to leave it open."

"She's coming here all the way from England? Weird," I say.

"Maybe she's going somewhere else as well." Tully sounds excited. He told us last night that he's always dreamed of having a guest ranch, once he got the traveling out of his bones. I'm not sure what I think. Tully already feels like family—that sounds like a cliché, but I swear it feels like we've known him longer than a week and a half. This woman will be a stranger. I'd way rather have the place to ourselves.

There's something else that bothers me, but I'm not sure what it is. I'm lying in bed later, tossing and turning because it's so muggy, when it comes to me. Tully said that Marion Wilson mentioned friends who were here ten years ago. But ten years ago the Double R wasn't a guest ranch. I know that because there was no guest book for that period. In fact, there was a gap of about six years. Even if Marion was out by a year or two, it couldn't be right.

Did Marion Wilson make a mistake? Or maybe there was a guest book and it just got lost. It's probably nothing, but it niggles away at me. It's a long time before I fall asleep.

Five

In the morning the sky is full of dark, foreboding clouds. I walk up to the end of Thurston Road. There's no sign of Van. While I wait for the school bus, I worry about what to do if he comes. I mean, the bus is going to be empty. So if he gets on first and goes to the back, am I supposed to follow him and sit beside him, or should I sit in the seat behind the bus driver again? I hate situations like this. I never know what to do.

Van races up on his bicycle at the last minute and has just enough time to hide it in the bushes before the bus comes. I end up getting on first. I sit down in the same seat I had yesterday and Van sits across the aisle. He wants to compare social studies homework.

For once I've got it done, and I let him copy some of my answers. "You're a life saver," he says, smiling, and I notice that he has a crooked front tooth.

We talk for a few minutes. The bus stops for two girls and a guy. Van gets up and moves to the back of the bus with them. He's probably sat in the same seat all year, but I still feel a tiny bit hurt. More kids get on and they all seem to go to the back. It gets noisier and noisier. There's a lot of laughing. A whiff of cigarette smoke drifts up the aisle. I resist the urge to turn around and see who it is. The bus driver yells, "Put it out NOW!" There's dead silence and then a few giggles.

I pull out my book and try to read.

❧

It's raining hard by the afternoon. Dad's waiting for me at the bus stop in his pickup truck. I mumble goodbye to Van, but Dad watches Van retrieve his bike, and he opens the window and says, "Why don't you throw that in the back and I'll give you a lift?"

"Sure," says Van. He's dripping by the time he slides onto the seat beside me.

It's steamy inside the truck. "The defogger's not working properly," says Dad as he wipes the windshield with his sleeve. The rain is coming down in sheets now and the wipers can't keep up.

Dad and Van chat like old friends while I sit silently. In the next few minutes I learn all kinds of things about Van: He has three sisters, all younger. His family lives in the house that Van's dad grew up in. His dad is a logger and his mom has a fabric shop in town and teaches quilting. Van's grand-parents live with them.

We go past the Double R Ranch sign and then, after about a kilometer, Van says, "Right here." A wooden sign hanging beside the road says *The Gallaghers*. Dad turns onto a narrow driveway that winds between rain-lashed trees. It's dark out, even though it's only four o'clock. A gray weathered house comes into view, with the lake, churned into small whitecaps, behind it. There's a swing set, the swings blowing in the wind, and a structure made out of red plastic blocks that looks like a playhouse.

When Van gets out, rain blows inside the truck, spattering the seat. He heaves his bike out of the back, shouts "Thanks" and disappears around the side of the house.

"Nice kid," says Dad, turning the truck around. "Is he in your grade?"

"Yeah," I say.

"Any of your classes?"

"Social studies," I mutter. I'm tensing up. Dad doesn't usually take an interest in my friends. In fact,

I don't think he's ever really noticed that I don't exactly have friends. I've always blamed it on him—all the moving around and changing schools. How can you make friends when you're only going to be around for a few months?

That's the excuse I use, anyway. But lately I've been starting to panic. Maybe it's something I'm doing. Or not doing. I tell myself I'm just out of practice. I *used* to have friends when we lived in the Valley.

Dad isn't giving up. "It's great that he lives so close."

"Right."

Dad looks at me sideways. "Don't be suspicious every time someone is nice to you."

The criticism stings and stupid tears form behind my eyes. What's wrong with Dad? And how does he know if Van's being nice or not?

"Drop it," I say, my voice sharp.

I mean it. I don't want to discuss Van. I don't even know if I like him.

Dad lifts both hands off the wheel and says, "Sorry."

I feel too tired to fight with Dad. I wipe the water off the seat with a rag that he keeps on the floor, and then I slide over to the window. The rain races in streaks down the glass. My thoughts turn to Renegade, wondering how he's doing in the storm.

When we get back to the ranch, Dad says he's going to get a bit more work done before dinner. He's right in the middle of tearing the old cabinets out of cabin five and only stopped to come and save me from getting soaked. I put on a raincoat, pull up the hood and hurry out to the barn. Renegade is in the shelter, staring out at the rain. He's wet, his black coat sleek, his tangled mane glistening with water drops. He's spread his hay around and tromped it into the ground, soggy and muddy. I lift up the blue tarp covering the bales of hay. There's a bale that I cut open this morning, the orange twine sprung to the side. I break off a flake and toss it in front of Renegade. I stay for five minutes, talking to him softly, and then go into the barn.

The rain is drumming on the metal roof, as loud as gunfire. It's dim but I find a switch on the wall, and when I flick it, the barn fills with bright light. I stand still for a minute, breathing in the smell.

Mom loved the smell too. I suck in my breath. Where did that come from? I don't even know if it's true. I try not to think about Mom. I don't really know what I'm supposed to feel. She left us to live with that trainer and that was a crummy thing to do.

The fact is, my memories of Mom are all screwed up. I remember Dad doing all those little-kid things like tucking me in at night or reading me a story.

I even remember him giving me my bath. But not Mom. She was always busy meeting with other trainers or judging horse shows or talking on the phone to clients. Did Mom even *think* about me after she left? I'll never know because she went and got herself killed and my world fell apart. Dad sold the stable and all the horses, including my horse Monty, who I adored, and we left.

I take a few deep breaths until I feel like myself again. Whatever that is. I decide I need a project, so I spend the next hour sorting through the pile of tack in the little room. I shake out saddle blankets, knocking out bits of grass and dirt and seeds, and stack them on racks. I move all the saddles to one side, straightening out girths, leaning them carefully against the wall. There's nothing really wrong with them that a bit of saddle soap won't fix. I hunt through the clutter on the shelves to see if I can find some. I dig through brushes, plastic curry combs, hoof picks, a tin of something called Hoof Maker, a bucket of rags, a bottle of mane detangler, some sponges. No saddle soap.

I clean up the mess on the shelves, finding a place for everything. I make a pile of things to throw away. Keeping busy makes me feel a lot better. When I'm finished, I survey the room. There's still lots to do but I've made a start. Suddenly I realize that it's quiet—

no more drumming on the roof. I go to the barn door and gaze out. Everything is dripping, but the clouds have torn apart and patches of watery blue sky are poking through. The air is fresh. I'm starving.

Six

It's lunch hour at school and for once I've got something to do. As soon as the bell rings, I head downtown to the tack store. It's four blocks away, right in the middle of the town, which is only about twelve blocks from end to end. A life-size model of a horse stands outside the store and there's a bulletin board by the door, covered with photographs of horses for sale and notices about riding camps and horse shows. I've been here once before, about two months ago, just to look around, but I never told Dad. I love everything in the store: the blankets with their bright Navaho designs; the gleaming saddles with intricate patterns tooled into the leather; the bright red, blue and green halters; even the rows of buckets on the floor filled with all kinds of brushes.

This time I have something I want to buy. I pick up a can of saddle soap and then, on an impulse, a brush with soft brilliant-pink bristles. When I leave the store, I check my watch. I have fifteen minutes until school starts for the afternoon, and there's something else I want to do.

I walk a couple more blocks to the museum. I've been thinking about that little girl who disappeared—Livia Willard—and I'm wondering if the museum might have some more newspaper clippings about her.

I pass kids going the other way, back to school, holding Slurpies, bags of chips and cans of soda. I avoid their eyes, though one girl says hi. Startled, I say hi back. The museum is in a small blue building that looks more like a house. A CLOSED sign hangs on the door. A smaller sign in the window lists the days and times that it's open, and I try to memorize them.

The school is quiet when I get back, the hallways empty. I'm late. I stash the brush and saddle soap in my locker and run to math class.

❧

It's Sunday afternoon and it's hot again, but not muggy like before. I'm lying on my stomach on a towel on our dock, propped up on my elbows, reading.

I just washed my hair and it's drying in the sun, spread over my shoulders. A motor thrums and I glance up. A boat is speeding toward the dock, two streams of white wake spreading out behind it.

It's Van. He cuts the motor when he gets close and drifts in to the dock. "Hey," he says.

"Hey," I say. I put my book down and sit up.

Van scrambles out and ties the boat to the side of the dock. He's barefoot, in cutoff jeans with no shirt. Something gold glints in the sun. It's a tiny cross on a chain around his neck. I've never known anyone my age who wore a cross. It's giving me all kinds of signals, but I'm not sure what they mean.

Van dangles his feet in the water, and I sit on my towel, my knees drawn up to my chin. We talk for a while about school, mostly which teachers we like and don't like, the same kind of nothing conversation we've been having every day while we wait for the school bus. Then Van says, right out of the blue, "You should try coming to the youth group in the fall."

I hide my surprise by slathering sunscreen on my legs. No one's invited me to anything for a long time. "What is it?" I ask.

"It's a group of kids that meet at the Baptist church."

"Oh," I say. Van has got to be kidding. I instantly remember the kids holding hands in a circle outside the school that day. The religious group.

Now I know where I've seen Van before, besides in social studies. He was the guy who smiled at me. "I don't think so."

"Why not?"

In a youth group, you'd probably be expected to talk about your problems to strangers. Like Alcoholics Anonymous or something. No way I'm doing that. But I can't say that to Van. "I don't believe in God." My voice sounds loud, too loud. I don't want Van to leave; I just don't want to join this group.

Van just shrugs. "So? Not everyone in the group goes to church. Pastor Jim won't care. He opens it up to anyone who wants to come."

"Who the heck is Pastor Jim?" I say. I grin. "And is that his real name?"

Van looks slightly ticked off. "He's in charge. Officially. But he's cool. He stays in the background. Let's us run it the way we want."

I'm not interested, I'm really not. But I ask anyway, "What kind of stuff do you do?"

"Hang out, watch movies, sometimes we go bowling or swimming or something. Just stuff."

Van sounds edgy now, and I wonder if I've offended him. The youth group might be okay; it's just not for me.

He stares at me. "You should try it," he repeats.

I don't like being pushed. "What? Stand around holding hands in a circle at school and looking weird?"

"It's just a prayer circle," says Van. "Just a way to get the day off to a good start. You wouldn't have to be part of it if you didn't want to."

"I like being alone," I say. "Honestly. Groups just aren't my thing. It's actually fun not having friends."

I don't know why I said that. It was supposed to be funny, but it sounds pathetic. Van's face is more transparent even than mine. He doesn't embarrass easily but he definitely looks annoyed. "I don't think sarcasm suits you," he says stiffly.

I'm tired of talking about this. I stand up and stretch. "Have you ever seen Renegade?" I ask.

"Who's Renegade?" says Van.

"A horse," I say. "Come on."

Van's impressed with Renegade.

We've brought apples, cut into slices, but Renegade still won't take them from my hand. We perch on the fence rail, watching him pace back and forth on the opposite side of the corral. The wind is blowing, tossing his mane.

"One of these days I'm going to start training him," I say. "When he gets used to me." I've been reading and rereading the articles I printed off the Internet, and I'm immersed in words like *pecking order* and *dominance* and *partnership*. But I'm still not sure how to start. I've been trying all week to get close enough to touch him, but he always skitters away.

Van nods seriously, as if he thinks I can really do it. "We have two ponies," he says. "My sisters ride."

"How about you?" I say. "Do you ride?"

"Nope. I've never been interested."

"I used to ride all the time," I say. I didn't plan to tell Van this. It just kind of spills out. "My mom and dad trained horses. Dad taught me how to ride when I was about three. I've got a picture of me sitting in front of him on his horse. When I was seven, they bought me an awesome horse called Monty."

"Really?" says Van. He sounds interested. Not annoyed anymore. "What happened?"

"What do you mean, what happened?"

"Well, your dad's fixing up cabins right now. That's not exactly training horses. And you've never said anything about your mom."

Now I'm really wishing that I had kept my mouth shut. I go for the condensed version. "Mom died in a riding accident when I was nine. We sold our stable. The rest is history."

I know I sound flippant but it's the only way I can deal with this. I've never talked about it to anyone. Everyone says it's better to let things out instead of bottling them up inside. I've never tested out that theory. Neither has Dad. I've already told Van more than I meant to. And I don't feel better. I just feel kind of scraped out inside.

"You must miss your mom," says Van.

"Actually I don't."

I've had enough. I jump down from the rail. Van jumps down beside me. "You must have hated giving up your horse."

I don't say anything.

"I'm sorry," he says.

I shrug. "Forget it. It doesn't matter anymore."

It's not exactly a lie, what I've told him, unless you can lie by leaving things out. There's no way I'm going to tell Van about Mom leaving us. It's complicated, way more complicated than Van thinks.

To his credit, he shuts up.

❧

Van ends up staying for dinner. He phones home from the lodge. I'm in the kitchen, slicing tomatoes for a salad, and Tully's frying hamburger meat for tacos.

I can hear Van saying, "Just tell Mom. Okay? It's none of your business. Just tell Mom."

"Sisters," he says when he gets off. "You're lucky you don't have any."

After we eat, Tully makes tea. We linger around the table and Tully tells stories about the Masai Mara in Africa. Dad and Van especially like hearing how it's the women who build the houses. They cover them with cow dung. Honestly.

"Come to think of it, the women do most of the work," says Tully.

"We should move there," says Dad, and Van snickers.

"Ha, ha," I say.

But I wouldn't mind going to Africa and seeing some of the things Tully's seen. I add that to my list of dreams—travel the world.

*

Van and I take Max and Bob for a walk after dinner. (Tinker is asleep on her bed, exhausted from chasing squirrels all afternoon, and won't budge.) We follow the dusty road that leads along the lakeshore, past the cabins. Between the trees, the lake glitters in the setting sun. A quavering cry breaks the stillness, sending goose bumps up my arms. Van says, "It's a loon.

There's a pair that nests here. They come every year. They nest on the island in the middle of the lake."

"I heard them one night," I say, "but I didn't know what it was."

The loon cries again, and this time there's an answering warble, far down the lake. I think about how cool it is that Van knows they come every year and where they nest. Dad and I will be gone in the winter, but Van will still be here. He's told me how he and his dad build a skating rink on the lake. It's hard to picture on this warm summer night, and I wish that I could see it.

Piles of rubble are heaped up outside cabin five, along with stacks of tarp-covered lumber and several sawhorses. Sawdust carpets the ground. We peek in the door. Most of the inside has been ripped out. The walls between the bedroom, the bathroom and the main room still stand, but there are no closets or cabinets or anything.

"It's going to be nice when it's finished," I say, remembering bits of Dad and Tully's conversation. "They're putting in pine siding and tile in the bathroom and brand-new appliances."

The sawdust makes Van sneeze, and we keep walking, all the way to cabin ten. This is where the road gets narrow and overgrown with grass until it disappears into the trees. It's as far as I've been.

"Tully said something about another old cabin at the end," I say. "It's kind of abandoned."

"I've seen it from the lake," says Van. "Let's see if we can find it."

No one's been past here in a car for years, I guess. Small bushes grow right in the middle of the road. In places the road seems to disappear altogether and we have to search in the grass for old tire ruts. We walk for a few minutes, brushing away mosquitoes, and then we spot the cabin, on the shore of a shallow marshy bay.

It's small, probably just one room. Like the other cabins, it's built out of logs, but it looks much older. It sags into the weeds as if it is tired. Lime green moss covers the logs in patches. Ragged holes gape between the shingles on the roof, and two of the windows are missing their glass.

The door is hanging by only one hinge. Van props it open and we go inside. The cabin is empty, except for a wooden table with a broken leg, and two chairs. There's an old wood-burning cookstove in one corner, with an enormous spiderweb suspended between the rusty stovepipe and the wall. Dried leaves are scattered across the floorboards, and the few windows that still have glass are thick with dust.

"A good project for your dad," says Van with a grin. He goes back outside, but I hang around for a few minutes. I try to picture someone living here, sitting at that table, eating a meal cooked on the stove.

Something catches my eye: marks gouged into the wood on the frame of the doorway. I trace them with my fingers. They look like letters but the wood has swollen around them and it's hard to make out what they are. There are four marks. A letter *S*, I think, maybe a *T*. Someone's name, scraped into the wood to prove they were here?

I go outside. At first I can't figure out what Van is doing. He's thrown his runners on the ground and rolled up his jeans. He's calf-deep in water. Then I realize he's standing on the remains of a dock submerged in the lake. He tips the half-rotten boards back and forth, waving his arms for balance.

"There's an old boat in the bushes over there," he says. "It's got some holes in it but I might be able to fix it up."

Bob has been for a swim and he gives a great shake, spraying my legs. I can hear Max somewhere close by, barking. I call him and a moment later he bursts out of the bushes, his tongue lolling.

Van rocks the dock again, bracing with his knees, and I say, "I'd laugh if you fell in."

"Not a chance." Van jumps to the shore. "The mosquitoes are horrible," he says. "Let's get out of here."

❧

It's dark when Van leaves. Dad's worried that he won't be able to see, but Van shows him the light on his boat. Besides, he says, he's grown up on this lake. He knows where all the hazards are.

Dad goes inside our cabin after Van leaves, but I stay on the dock. I hear the thrum of the boat's motor long after Van disappears into the darkness. When I finally go inside to get ready for bed, I walk over to the dresser in my tiny bedroom and look at a photograph of me perched in front of Dad on his horse Skipper. I look about four years old. I'm wearing a helmet and Dad is wearing a cowboy hat that shades his face. His arms are wrapped right around me, and I'm grinning. I tell myself I can remember those rides with Dad, but I can't really. For the first time I wonder who took the photograph.

Seven

A small blue car is parked outside cabin two. I spot it just before supper the next day, on my way back to our cabin from the barn. The guest that Tully was expecting must have arrived while I was with Renegade.

I brush bits of hay off my jeans before I go inside. Then I change my T-shirt, wash the horse smell off my hands and head to the lodge.

Tully wants everything to be perfect for his first official guest. At the end of the long table, he has laid four places, with woven place mats and blue-handled cutlery I haven't seen before. Wild lupins and brilliant Indian paintbrush fill a tall white vase.

He's lifting a pie with a brown-sugar-sprinkled crust out of the oven when I come in. I inhale a delicious breath of apples and cinnamon.

A woman is standing in front of the wall beside the fireplace, her back to me, looking at some of Tully's photographs.

"There you are, Thea," says Tully, setting the pie on a rack. "I'd like you to meet Mrs. Wilson."

"Oh, please, call me Marion," says the woman, turning around. She has a crisp English accent and is small and kind of birdlike, with short gray hair. She looks like she's in her sixties. I was expecting someone younger. She's dressed neatly in pressed blue jeans, a pink sweatshirt and white running shoes.

Marion walks across the room to shake hands with me. "Tully's been telling me about you," she says. Her eyes are bright blue, and up close I can see fine wrinkles in her skin. "It's lovely to meet you."

"It's great to meet you too," I say. Marion Wilson seems nice, and I can't think of a single reason why she would have lied about her friends staying here ten years ago. I decide that Tully must have got it wrong, or maybe the ranch *was* operating then and there just aren't any guest books from those years.

Dad arrives and Tully makes the introductions again.

Dad and Marion talk about the flight from England and the drive up from Vancouver. I gravitate to Tully's Africa photographs. Every time I look at them, I notice something new. This time it's the soft downy manes on the backs of the baby cheetahs.

At dinner, most of the conversation is about Italy. Marion has traveled there a lot, and she and Tully have been to some of the same places. Dad says that Italy is somewhere he has always wanted to go. For a moment I look at Dad with new eyes. This is something I never knew about him. The talk drifts to Italian wines and it turns out that Dad knows something about those too.

After a while, Marion changes the subject. "I'll join you for dinner and I'll take you up on that offer of a bag lunch, but I'll pass on breakfast. And I certainly don't need maid service in my cabin or anything like that." Her voice is brisk.

Tully looks disappointed. He's so excited about being a host. "How about clean towels every few days?"

"That would be fine. And I would like the use of a boat while I'm here," says Marion.

"No problem," says Tully. "We've got canoes and a couple of small boats with electric motors. Thea can show you."

Marion smiles at me. "That would be lovely."

"I'm sorry we can't offer you riding," says Tully. "You'll have to come back next year."

"Oh, I'm afraid my riding days are over," says Marion quickly.

"You used to ride?" I say, for the first time really focusing on the conversation.

"A lot. I had a bad fall about ten years ago. The doctor warned me that if I fell again, I'd do some serious damage to my back. But until then I rode almost every day."

"What kind of horses?" I ask.

"Thoroughbreds," says Marion. "Steeplechasers." There's a slight pause and then she adds, "It was my aunt and uncle's business, and when they died I took it over."

I'm totally impressed. "Did you race?"

Marion smiles. "We had jockeys to do the racing. But I started lots of young colts. And I rode them on training rides."

"I'm planning on getting into breeding," says Tully proudly. "Quality quarter horses. I'm researching bloodlines. It's always been a dream of mine."

"That's exciting," says Marion, "but a big undertaking."

"And all new to me," confesses Tully. "Ah well, I like a challenge."

There's a scraping sound as Dad abruptly pushes back his chair. He mutters something about banging in a few more nails.

"What about apple pie?" says Tully.

"Later," says Dad, and then he's gone. For what seems like a long time, no one speaks. My cheeks flush.

Dad sounded so rude. I wonder what Marion is thinking.

"Homemade apple pie," she says, breaking the silence. "You're spoiling me."

I dig into my pie, which is still warm. Tully says he'll bring the coffee out to the porch, and I gather up the dirty dishes and take them to the dishwasher. For a second, I almost tell Marion Wilson about Renegade. Then I change my mind. I'm not sure I want to share him yet.

ℒ

The light on my watch tells me it's 2:00 AM. Sweat soaks my back and my heart is racing. I take a few deep breaths, relief flooding me as I realize that I was dreaming. That's all it is. A bad dream.

It felt so real, but already the details are fading. I try to piece the dream back together in my mind, grasping blurred images. I remember we were looking for Livia Willard, the little girl who went missing. It's all mixed up because she disappeared nearly sixty years ago, but we were all there—Tully, Dad, Van, me and a shadowy person who I think might have been Marion Wilson.

In the part of the dream that I remember clearly, we were standing in a marshy spot beside the lake—

not anywhere that I recognized, but I think it must have been Gumboot Lake—and someone was shouting that they'd found something. It was a pink running shoe with a bunny on it. Then somehow I was swimming underwater and there were weeds everywhere, pulling at my legs and arms. And then the weeds turned into hair, blond curls swirling in the water, and I saw a pale face.

I waded onto shore, the weeds still dragging at me like skinny arms. I could hear someone sobbing. It sounded like a young child, but I couldn't see anyone. And then the dream got weirder and somehow I was in a forest and a person was standing beside a tree. It was the girl in the photograph, the older sister. I frowned, trying to remember her name. Esta. Her face was expressionless and her eyes were blank, but I knew she was watching me.

"Where's Livia?" I said.

"Livia is dead," she replied.

That's when I woke up.

I push back the damp sheets and climb out of bed. I pour myself a glass of water at the kitchen sink, quietly so I don't wake Dad. The window over the sink is open, letting in cool air, and moths beat at the screen with their silvery wings. It's harder and harder to hold on to the dream, though one question nags at me:

Did Livia drown? That must have been one of the first things the police thought of. They would have searched all along the lakeshore. Is that where they found her?

Something catches my eye outside. It's a light, shining through the trees. For a second I can't figure it out, but then I realize it must be coming from Marion Wilson's cabin. I watch for a few minutes, wondering what she's doing. When I turn to go back to bed, shivering with goose bumps, the light is still on.

Eight

Van has asked me to his house for dinner. It's not a date. How could it be when his whole family is going to be there? His mom, his dad, his three sisters and both his grandparents. But it's the first time a boy has ever asked me to do anything, and I take a pathetically long time to get ready. I've discarded four tops when I hear Van talking to Dad outside on the dock. In a panic I pull on a black halter top (the one I started with in the first place) and head outside.

Van has come for me in his boat. It's Wednesday; school tomorrow. He promises Dad that he'll bring me back before dark, even though I remind them that it's the last week before summer vacation starts, and we're not doing anything in class anyway. I scramble into the bow of the boat and Van swings it around and guns the motor. We surge forward toward the middle of the lake, tiny waves beating against the tipped-up bow, and my hair blowing in the wind.

Marion Wilson is just coming back in to shore in a small blue boat. She's sitting very erect in the stern, her hand on the tiller of the motor, and she's wearing a straw hat. I wave at her and she waves back as she heads toward the dock in front of her cabin. I wonder idly if she has been out all day, if that's why she wanted a bag lunch.

"That's Marion Wilson," I tell Van. "She's a guest from England."

Van nods. He picks up speed. I've explored in one of the canoes a few times, but I've always stayed near the ranch, going only as far down the lake as a small island covered in scraggly trees and a lot of bleached gray wood. Van shouts out something as we fly past the island, and I turn around so I can hear him. He slows the motor a little and says, "That's Spooky Island. I used to build forts there all the time when I was a little kid. My sisters still play there."

"Why is it called Spooky Island?" I ask.

Van shrugs. "Don't remember. Maybe because all that dead wood kind of looks like bones."

He's cut the motor right down until we're barely idling. The breeze dies suddenly and the lake turns to glass. I dangle my hand over the side of the boat and scoop up a handful of cold water. It trickles through my fingers like silk. It's peaceful out here. Blue sky. Green water.

Van seems to be making up his mind about something. "Do you want to see something cool?" he says finally.

"Sure," I say.

Van lets the throttle right out and we slice across the smooth lake, heading for the far side. The shore is much steeper on this side; dense forest, with the occasional outcropping of bare rock, climbs straight up to the sky. We cruise along the edge for a while. Then, in the mouth of a small bay carpeted with pale green lily pads, Van turns the motor off and lifts the propeller up out of the water. He slides to the seat in the middle of the boat, where he picks up a set of oars. "The weeds and stuff will clog up the propeller," he explains. "We've got to row from here."

With strong thrusts of the oars, Van noses the boat into the lily pads and across the bay to the shore. The lily pads make a rustling sound against the bottom of the boat; it's the only sound other than the splash of the oars. We're approaching a cliff with scraggly trees growing out of bare rock. Just when I think we're going to bump right into it, I see what Van is heading for: a slit in the cliff wall, just wide enough for the boat. We glide through into a place of shadows and dark water. A secret pool.

"It doesn't go very far," says Van. "It's just like a little inlet. But I like it because if you don't know it's here, you'd never find it."

The long narrow pool is cut out of the cliff. There are steep banks, rimmed with trees, on either side, and at the end are slopes of rust-colored boulders covered in patches of lime green moss. It's dank and cold, the water almost black. A different kind of lake weed grows here, hanging in tangled brown clumps just below the surface of the water.

"It's awesome in here," I say, shivering, "but kind of creepy too."

I pick up a clump of the slippery brown weed and hold it, dripping, over the water. We sit still for a few minutes, and then Van says, "I just wanted you to see this. You've got goose bumps. Let's get back out into the sun."

When we come back out into the little bay, the sun is dazzling, bouncing off the lily pads. The warmth feels glorious on my bare arms and legs.

I just wanted you to see this. As we fly down the lake, I ponder the amazing news flash that Van has chosen *me* to be his friend.

❧

"Do you know how old I am?" says Van's grandfather. He's sitting beside me at the dining-room table. He's a thin man with wispy gray hair, and skin mottled with brown spots.

Van's house is great. Like the lodge at the ranch, it's filled with photographs. They're propped up on tables and clutter the walls, but they're different from Tully's; they're of family, and there are tons of school photographs of Van and his sisters. There are also more books than I've ever seen in one house, crammed onto shelves that climb all the way to the ceiling.

We're about to eat. Van's grandmother is a large, red-cheeked woman with gray hair in a long braid. She was baking biscuits when we arrived and she's still wearing an apron dusted with flour. She's sitting on my other side, and Van is beside her. His three sisters sit facing us. Dawn is ten, Ginny is eight and Katie is six. Except for size, they're very alike: freckles, blond hair and huge brown eyes. We met earlier out in the field, admiring and feeding carrots to the two ponies and throwing sticks for the golden retriever, Prince.

"How old do you think I am?" Van's grandfather persists.

"Um, I don't know," I say.

Katie giggles.

"Eighty-nine," he says with a grin. "I'm having my ninetieth birthday on September sixth. We're having a big party."

"With all the bells and whistles," says Van's dad. He's moving around the table, filling glasses with water from a pottery jug.

At the other end of the table, Van's mother glances around and says, "I think we have everything."

Van's parents have told me to call them by their first names, Martin and Jane, and Van's grandparents insist on Heb and May, but I'm feeling a little uncomfortable so I don't call them anything. My plate is heaped with food: fried chicken, potato salad, green beans, creamed corn and a biscuit. I'll never be able to eat it all. I pick up the biscuit nervously, break it open and spread some butter on it.

I've taken a bite when it hits me like a cement truck. No one else is eating. They're all waiting for something. The girls stare at me and then look at their mother to see what she's going to do. My cheeks flame.

Jane says in this smooth voice, "Dawn, how would you like to say grace tonight?"

Grace. Crap. I should have known. I want to slide under the table. I want to completely and utterly disappear. A wad of biscuit is trapped in my mouth, and I'm sure everyone hears me swallow.

Dawn sucks in her breath. "Thank you, God, for our meal and thank you for having Thea come and visit us. Amen."

"Amen," echo six more voices around the table.

Everyone is eating now and the moment has passed, but I still feel like a moron. I'm also mad at Van for not warning me.

The conversation is dominated by Van's sisters, who all have stories to tell from their day at school. I'm happy to sit quietly, trying to get used to so much family.

In between the main course and dessert (I wait cautiously until Van swallows a spoonful of ice cream in case there's some kind of second grace), Van's grandfather falls asleep. His head tilts forward and he starts to snore gently. No one else seems to notice, or maybe they're used to it. I worry that he might topple over sideways but after a few minutes he wakes up. His faded blue eyes survey the table. "What are we talking about?" he says politely.

For a second, Jane hesitates. "I was just asking Thea about the ranch," she says.

"We used to work at the ranch," says Heb. "I was a handyman and May was the cook. But I don't remember when."

"It was a long time ago," says May gently.

And then from somewhere Heb produces a nugget of information. "I was thirty-one years old when I started there. Your grandmother, girls, was twenty-seven. When was that?"

There is a pause. I sense that Van's parents and May are trying to protect Heb from something. What?

"In the nineteen-fifties," May finally says.

"I don't like Van going down there," says Heb. He turns to Van and says sharply, "You're not to go there anymore. They'll blame you."

"Grandpa," says Van.

"They never found her," says Heb. "Never. They searched everywhere but not a trace."

Livia. He must be talking about Livia.

A tickle runs up my spine. Van's grandparents were at the ranch when Livia disappeared, they must have been. And then something shifts in my brain as Heb's words sink in. *Not a trace.* For some reason I'd been sure that Livia had eventually been found. Maybe she had wandered away into the woods. Or maybe she had drowned and they had found her body.

"Never found who, Grandpa?" says Ginny.

"Never mind now, Ginny," says Jane.

And then Heb's delicate hands, which were folded in his lap, start to flap. He says in a bewildered voice, "Why are we talking about the ranch?"

"It doesn't matter," says Jane. She looks at Martin and he stands up.

"It's okay, Dad," he says. "I'm going to set you up in your sitting room with your tea."

Heb allows himself to be led away from the table.

"What's wrong with Grandpa?" says Dawn, her eyes sharp.

Van's grandmother smoothes her hands on her apron and says calmly, "It's just his dementia. He's mixing up the past and the present. He'll be fine in the morning."

Dawn persists. "Is Van allowed to go to the ranch?"

"Of course he's allowed," says Jane. "I'm sorry about all that, Thea."

"That's okay," I say.

"We're awfully proud of Heb," says Jane. "He's usually as sharp as a tack. He knows so much about everything. He must have done too much today."

"He's never said that before," said Van. "About me not going to the ranch."

For a second I think May is going to tell us something. Then her eyes flicker over the girls, who are finishing their ice cream, and she says simply,

"There's nothing to worry about. Van, why don't you take Thea to see Grandpa's birds? That will put him right."

⤫

Heb and May's sitting room is at the back of the house. Heb's sunk deep in an armchair with a red plaid blanket across his knees, drinking tea. He's surrounded by birds: ducks and geese and a tall great blue heron, woodpeckers, robins and tiny little birds that I don't recognize. They're carved out of wood and delicately painted in vibrant reds and blues, pale smoky grays, rich cinnamon. They perch on tables and shelves and the sill of a big window that looks out on the lake. They take my breath away, they're so beautiful.

"Did you make these?" I say.

"Every last one," says Heb proudly. He sets his teacup down and wipes his mouth with a napkin. "I don't carve anymore. Hands are too stiff with this darn arthritis."

"They're incredible," I say.

"Grandpa had a show once," says Van proudly. "In the gallery in town. They asked him to take the show to Vancouver but he didn't want to move the birds so far."

"They belong here at Gumboot Lake," says Heb. "There are no foreigners among them, just everyday birds you can see around here."

"Can I touch them?" I ask.

"Oh yes," says Heb.

I pick up a little bird that is the color of a summer sky. "I love this one," I say.

"Mountain bluebird," says Heb. "The male. It's a pretty little thing."

He gets up stiffly and walks around the room with me, naming birds: northern flicker, blue-winged teal, wood duck and a ruby-throated hummingbird that fits in the palm of my hand.

I'm amazed at how good his memory is now. "I've spent my whole life watching birds," he says. His eyes twinkle. "Tried to get my grandson here interested but no luck. Now young Ginny, she's got the bug. I'm starting her on a carving of a mallard."

"I think they're wonderful," I say.

"Well, it's a hobby that's kept me out of trouble."

Heb is tiring. He sinks back into his chair and pulls the blanket around his thin legs.

"We'll leave you now, Grandpa," says Van.

"Thank you for showing me your birds," I say.

"Goodbye, Thea." Heb puts out his hand for me to shake. It feels as fragile as the tiny hummingbird.

"Goodbye," I say.

"You come in and see me before you go to bed, Van, and we'll have that game of chess." Heb's grin is wicked. "My boy and I are at a draw, Thea, three games to three. Tonight's the night I whump him."

On the way back in the boat, I tell Van about the newspaper article about Livia Willard. He's amazed that he has never heard of her before. We're both sure that his grandfather was talking about Livia at dinner. In his muddled-up mind, did he think that Van would get blamed for Livia's disappearance?

We decide to go to the museum on Friday to see if we can find any more newspaper clippings. The museum is open from one till four, so we'll have to skip out of school. It's the last day so it'll just be pizza and a movie anyway. Since Van and I usually ignore each other at school, I almost make a sarcastic remark about Van preferring to hang out with his youth-group friends instead of coming with me to the museum.

I bite my lip and keep my mouth shut. I'm getting smarter.

Nine

It's Thursday after supper and something amazing has just happened. I've lured Renegade into the round pen. First I opened the pen's metal gate, and then I got a bucket of grain. I walked slowly down the middle of the corral, shaking the bucket so the grain rattled. Renegade followed me at a wary distance, unable to resist, right through the gate and into the pen! I dumped the grain on the ground, then slid back around Renegade with the empty bucket and shut the gate.

Now I am outside and he is inside.

I take a deep breath. I'm not so cocky now about trapping him, just apprehensive.

In my pocket is a crumpled piece of paper. I don't need to take it out to read it. I know what I wrote.

Control movement.
Control direction.

Those are the two things I need to work on first.

Renegade finishes his grain. He trots around the pen, his head lowered to the ground, blowing through his nose. He makes three or four circles and then he stops and presses his nose against the metal pipes. They're too high for him to stick his head over. I wonder if he's feeling as nervous as I am.

I pick up a coiled rope that I've laid on the ground, ready for this moment. It's soft and about twenty feet long. I felt a small burst of triumph when I found it in the tack room. It's exactly what the articles from the Internet say I need.

That's all. Just a rope. I bite my lip and slide the latch on the gate. I slip inside the round pen and shut the gate. It clangs and Renegade jumps. I move to the middle of the pen, my eyes on Renegade. He swings his butt toward me and flattens his ears.

Control movement.

That's where I'll start. My plan is to make Renegade move. Anywhere, it doesn't matter where. As long as he moves when I tell him to. That will establish my leadership. Or, as one article said, I will be the lead mare in this tiny herd of ours. Horses need a leader. They feel safer, more secure. That's the theory, anyway.

I hurl the end of the rope toward his butt. I don't mean to throw so hard. It smacks against his flank and wraps around his back leg.

He kicks out hard. The rope jerks from my hand and dirt sprays my face. I duck instinctively. He explodes into a fast gallop, streaking around the pen as if he is being chased by a thousand demons. I'm terrified he'll fall or crash into the pipe walls. The pen is small, too small for this speed. The eye I can see rolls in fear. Hooves churn the ground into dust. Flanks turn sleek with sweat.

I am rooted to the ground, my legs weak. Every part of me says to stay out of his way. Everything I've read leaves my head. I've no idea how to stop him. I'm sure he's going to kill himself. Or kill me.

He gallops around and around, his hindquarters surging, his hooves drumming rhythmically. Dust and the pungent smell of his sweat choke my nostrils.

I'm in awe of his power.

I think he's gone crazy.

I remember more words. *Round pen work is not about mindlessly racing a horse around in circles. A horse that is not fit can run to exhaustion or death.*

A random thought jumps into my head: Dad would know what to do.

Change direction.

That's the second step. Now that he's moving, I have to tell him which direction.

I'm terrified to try. I'm certain I'll be trampled. So I do nothing.

After what seems like forever, Renegade slows to a canter and then a trot. *Control movement. Change direction.* Since I tossed the rope, Renegade has been the boss. I'm nowhere near being the lead mare. Renegade knows it too. He kicks out in my direction—hard, resentful—and then stands still, his sides heaving, blowing through his flared nostrils. He won't look at me.

The dust settles. I stare at him, my heart racing. Flecks of foam speckle his black muzzle.

Shaken, I open the gate. I leave it open for Renegade. I pick up the rope and loop it over my shoulder. Then I grab the empty grain bucket and escape back to the barn. I need to think. I need a better plan.

Ten

When Van and I get to the museum at twenty after one, one of those plastic clocks saying *Back in Ten Minutes* is hanging in the window. We go to the 7-Eleven for Cokes and guzzle them on the hot, sunny sidewalk in front of the museum. I'm filled with the joy that comes on the last day of school.

An old rust-speckled car pulls up to the curb and a woman gets out, calling, "Sorry to keep you waiting." She has spiky black hair sticking out of a brightly colored bandanna and piercings on her nose and eyebrow. She walks around to the passenger side and lifts a small blond boy out of a car seat.

"Had to pick up Jeremy at the day care," she explains. "He's not feeling well. I'm Hana."

Hana unlocks the door and turns on lights. We're in a small room filled with glass cases; a display of old-fashioned dresses stands against one wall. "There's a lot more to see in the other rooms," says Hana. She sets Jeremy on a blanket in the corner with a couple of picturebooks and a plastic container of Cheerios. "Any questions, just ask." She eyes our Cokes. "Please leave the drinks out here though."

We set the cans on the counter. "We're wondering if you have any old newspapers," I say.

Hana frowns. "How old?"

"From the fifties," I say.

"We don't actually have whole newspapers," says Hana. "But we have file folders of clippings. You know, stuff that happened in the town that was interesting. I don't know how far back they go, but you can look. If you can't find what you want, you might check at the newspaper office. I think they keep archives."

She directs us to several tall gray filing cabinets in a tiny room behind the counter. It's more like a walk-in storage closet, filled with boxes of books, tattered magazines, an old clock and a bulging bag of clothes. There's a kettle and a box of tea beside a sink.

"I'm new here," says Hana, "and I'm not sure how things were filed. You might have to do some digging."

The first filing cabinet is crammed with folders with headings like *Arctic Animals, The Galapagos, Aviation, Greek Architecture.* I peek inside a few of them; they're filled with articles and pictures cut out of glossy magazines. The second filing cabinet has newspaper clippings, but they're all recent: municipal elections, the campaign to build a new recreation center, closures at the mill. I'm starting to feel discouraged. Maybe the newspaper archives would have been better.

"In here!" Van bursts out. He's been rummaging through the filing cabinet beside me. "This goes way back." And then "Aha!"

He produces a tan file folder with *Livia Willard* written in black felt pen on the tab. I can't believe our luck. I had started to think we were crazy.

Inside are five newspaper clippings, held together with a paper clip. I spread them out on the table in the front room. We sit down and I pass Van the article dated July 9, 1954. The headline reads *DOUBLE TRAGEDY AT CARIBOO GUEST RANCH.* It's the same one that I found in the guest book.

I pick up another article and start to read.

July 10, 1954

SEARCH FOR MISSING GIRL CONTINUES

An extensive search for four-year-old Livia Willard, who disappeared the afternoon of July 7 at the Double R Guest Ranch, continues. Police and volunteers have searched the shoreline of Gumboot Lake and the forested area around the ranch. The police are not ruling out foul play. Beth Ryerson, sister of Wayne Willard, arrived from England on July 9 to be with her two young nieces, eight-year-old Iris and fourteen-year-old Esta, and her daughter Melissa, who has been visiting the family. She says she would like to thank everyone who is working so hard to find Livia and that the family wishes privacy at this time. Funeral services for Livia's parents, Wayne and Joan Willard, killed in a car accident as they returned to the ranch, will be held in North Vancouver on July 14.

There's not much in there that I don't already know. I pick up the next article. The headline catches my attention.

ARREST IN WILLARD
DISAPPEARANCE

There has been a breakthrough in the case of the missing four-year-old girl, Livia Willard, who was last seen on the afternoon of July 7 at the Double R Ranch. Livia's fourteen-year-old sister, Esta Willard, has come forward and said that shortly before Livia disappeared she saw her sister in the front seat of a truck belonging to Heb Gallagher, an employee at the ranch. Gallagher has worked at the ranch for the past four years as a maintenance and general handy man. His wife, May Gallagher, is the cook. After extensive interrogation, police have charged Gallagher with abduction. He is being held without bail.

My first thought, after the shock of seeing his grandparents' names, is for Van. I would give anything for him not to know this, but it's too late. He has already picked up the clipping and is reading.

"Oh my god," he whispers. "Grandpa." He stares at me, stricken. "This is awful."

I feel sick. I wish I'd never suggested coming here. I have a horrible feeling that I have disturbed something that was meant to stay buried. "Look, maybe we should—," I start to say.

"No," says Van. "I need to know."

The next clipping is only a few lines.

July 17, 1954

CHARGES IN WILLARD CASE DROPPED

Charges against Heb Gallagher, an employee at the Double R Ranch, have been dropped. Police have declined to comment, saying only that he remains a person of interest.

"That was three days later," says Van. He sounds shaken. He's probably imagining what those three days must have been like for his grandpa.

There is one final clipping. The paper looks newer, the print not as faded. I check the date. It's more than twenty years after the other articles. We read it together.

August 2, 1979

CASE STILL ACTIVE AFTER TWENTY-FIVE YEARS

Police have reopened several cases of interest in the area, including the disappearance of Livia Willard in 1954. Four-year-old Livia disappeared twenty-five years ago on July 7, 1954, from the Double R Guest Ranch, where she was vacationing with her parents, Joan and Wayne Willard, her sisters, Iris and Esta, and her English cousin Melissa. Despite a thorough search, the little girl was never found. The police are interested in speaking to anyone who lived in the area in 1954. A local man, a former employee of the guest ranch, was questioned extensively at the time. He was charged but released after a few days. Now fifty-eight years old, he remains a person of interest and has been requestioned by the police. He claimed that he was fishing at Marmot Lake when Livia disappeared and has always maintained his innocence.

Van looks sick. I wish we had never come. My head spins, but it always comes back to the same thing. It's insane trying to connect Livia's disappearance with Heb, who carves beautiful birds and loves his grandchildren.

Van shoves the newspaper articles back into the folder. "Let's get out of here," he says.

❧

We don't talk as we walk back to school. A horn honks; it's Dad in his pickup truck. He pulls over to the curb. He says that he's been in town picking up some building supplies and that he'll give us a ride home. I wonder if Van would rather take the bus on the last day so he can say goodbye to his friends. I'm going to tell him that I don't mind if he does, but he says, "That'd be great, thanks," and we both climb in.

As we drive out to Gumboot Lake, Dad and Van talk across me about where all the good fishing lakes are. Van is polite and answers Dad's questions, but I'm sure that he's still feeling as stunned as I am. I stare through the windshield at the road. I can't stop thinking about Van's grandfather and Livia.

Eleven

I get out at Van's house and tell Dad I'll be home for dinner. Prince, the family's golden retriever, gallops across the grass to meet us. I kneel down and bury my face in his neck.

Dawn and Ginny are in front of the barn, brushing the ponies. I go over to say hi and then join Van in the kitchen.

Van's mom is making strawberry jam. Gleaming jars are lined up on the counter, and a huge pot simmers on the stove. "Hi, Thea," she says. "Help yourself." I pick a fat strawberry out of a cardboard flat and pop it into my mouth.

Van is pacing back and forth like a tiger in a cage. I can feel the tension coming off him in waves.

. "I *know*, Mom," he says finally in a tight voice. "I *know* about Grandpa and that girl that went missing."

Jane stops stirring the pot and stares at Van.

"Why didn't anyone ever tell me?" he says fiercely.

"Oh, Van," says Jane. "How did you find out?"

"It's my fault," I say. "I found a newspaper article about Livia. And I wanted to know what happened to her. So we went to the museum and we read about it there."

"I just want to know why you didn't tell me," Van says.

A voice says quietly, "We didn't tell you because we promised your grandpa that you would never know."

It is May, in the doorway.

"I don't want you upsetting Grandma," says Jane.

"Nonsense," says May.

She asks Van and me to join her for tea in her and Heb's sitting room.

"It's a good time to talk," she says. "Heb has gone to town with Van's dad to do some chores."

We go into the sitting room. I marvel again at Heb's birds. They are so lifelike. They look as if they might burst into flight at any minute. I stroke the feathers on a duck while May pours tea into china cups. She opens a round tin and puts some cookies on a plate.

"Van is right," May says. "He should have been told. After all, we have nothing to hide. What do you want to know?"

"Everything," says Van.

May is silent. I wonder if she is doing what I do, picking out the bits she wants to tell, deciding what should remain a secret. After all, some things are nobody's business.

"First of all," says May finally, "the charges were dropped. There was no evidence whatsoever that Grandpa was involved. It was just the story of a mixed-up teenager."

"That's so unfair," says Van.

"Of course it is." May folds her hands, her tea forgotten. "We knew the Willard family well. They came to the ranch every year, right from when Livia was a baby. They always came in the beginning of July and stayed for two weeks. Esta was the oldest, Iris was in the middle and then there was little Livia. The family always took the same cabin, that big one with two bedrooms and a loft."

A slight shiver runs over me. That sounds like the cabin Dad and I are living in. I wonder if all three girls slept in my room. I imagine them in old-fashioned nightgowns, whispering until they fell asleep.

"The year Livia disappeared, they had their niece from England with them," says May. "Her name was Melissa. She was a great rider. Her parents owned some kind of fancy riding stable in England. The day Livia disappeared, Melissa went on a trail ride all afternoon and left the two younger girls with Esta."

Disapproval sharpens May's voice. "Melissa was in charge. She should have stayed with the girls. Especially Livia. She was only four."

I try to remember exactly what the newspaper articles said. "The girls' parents had gone back to Vancouver," I say.

"That's right," says May. "I can't remember why. Some kind of family emergency, I suppose." She frowns. "They didn't want to leave the girls at first. There was quite a to-do, especially about whether Livia should go with her parents. She was so young. Wayne wanted to take her to Vancouver. He adored her. He was absolutely crazy about her. And he was worried."

"What was he so worried about?" I ask.

"Livia suffered from asthma. Her asthma had been particularly bad that summer. I remember the poor little mite struggling to catch her breath. But she'd been better the last few days, and in the end they decided to leave her at the ranch. I think they thought she'd be happier there."

"If Livia had gone with her parents, everything would have been different," says Van. He sounds bitter.

"If Wayne had had his way, she would have. But Joan said to leave her at the ranch with Melissa. After all, Melissa was in her twenties. She wasn't a child."

May pauses. "Don't get me wrong. Livia was the apple of her mother's eye too. You see, she was Joan's only child."

"But what about Esta and Iris?" I say.

"They weren't Joan's. She was their stepmother. Wayne had been married before. Esta and Iris's mother died of cancer."

"So Livia was their half sister," I say.

"Yes," says May. "Joan was younger than Wayne by quite a number of years. She was ecstatic to have her own child. She was always fixing Livia up nicely. Those curls weren't natural. Oh no. Joan used to set Livia's hair every night. I used to think it would be nice if she spent a little bit of that time on Iris. Iris had straight mousy hair and a little peaked face, but she was appealing in her own way. Esta was such an unattractive girl. She couldn't help it. She had what we used to call a pudding face. And she was big for her age. Awkward."

"Did Esta and Iris mind that Livia got so much attention?"

"Esta did. Definitely. I don't think Iris noticed so much. She was crazy about the horses and spent a lot of time at the barn. I remember thinking—

after their parents were killed in the accident and their aunt took them back to England with her—that at least Iris would have all those horses to console her."

"But Esta minded?"

"Oh yes, Esta was fiercely jealous of Livia. I saw her push her right down in the dirt more than once when she thought no one was looking." May sighs. "Esta bullied Iris too, and I think both girls were afraid of her. It's a terrible thing, to be afraid of your own sister."

Van speaks now, his voice tight with impatience. "The day Livia disappeared. What happened?"

May doesn't answer for a long time. Then she says, "Esta was in a foul temper that afternoon. She complained all through lunch. She didn't think it was fair that she had to look after Livia and Iris while Melissa was having fun riding. Livia could be a handful and she was fussing—missing her mother and father I expect."

May's blue-veined hand trembles. She sets her teacup down and it rattles in the saucer. "Esta said they went for a walk," she says softly. "I always suspected it was to that old cabin at the end of the road. It was never used for guests so it was empty. Esta used it as a kind of playhouse, and sometimes she made Iris go there with her."

"The cabin's still there," I say. "Van and I found it."

"Really?" says May. "Well, the girls weren't supposed to go to the old cabin that summer, and according to Esta, they didn't. But Esta, quite frankly, was not a truthful girl. She said they played on that little beach toward the end of the road, and then Iris and Livia went back to the cabin they were staying in. Esta insisted that the two of them left together. Esta stayed a little longer. She said that when she got back to their cabin, Iris was asleep on the bed. She woke Iris up and asked her where Livia was and Iris didn't know."

"But Esta changed her story," says Van. "She said she saw Livia in Grandpa's truck."

"Yes, she did say that," says May slowly. Her eyes fill with shadows. The lines in her skin seem deeper. "It was a confusing time. Melissa was hysterical when she got back from the ride. She blamed herself. Everyone was hunting for Livia. And then, of course, that night we got the terrible news that the girls' parents had been killed. The police said that Wayne crossed the center line. He must have been in an awful state, driving back to the ranch knowing that Livia was missing."

"Esta changed her story," Van persists, his voice angry. "Why did people believe her?"

May hesitates, as if she is choosing her words carefully. "She didn't really change her story. She just added to it. She always insisted that Livia had gone back with Iris. The police said that, with all the trauma, Esta's memory would come in bits and pieces. They thought that perhaps Livia had wandered away when Iris fell asleep and that Esta had seen her in Heb's truck when she was walking back to their cabin."

"What did Iris say?"

"Iris?" May frowns. "All I remember is Iris crying. Crying and crying and crying. She was only eight, and she was devastated. She screamed when the police tried to talk to her."

"So it was just Esta's word," says Van. "What about Grandpa?"

"He never saw Livia that day. He took the afternoon off and drove up to Marmot Lake to throw in his fishing line. He wasn't even here. The problem was, no one saw him leave. And there was no one at Marmot Lake, so there was no one to give him an alibi. We were expecting a big crowd the next week, all the cabins full, and I was baking all afternoon, trying to get a store of pies and muffins and such in the freezers. So I didn't see him leave either. The ranch was quiet—most of the guests were off on the trail ride. When Heb got back, everyone was looking for Livia and he joined in the search right away. He was upset, terribly upset, thinking that something bad might have happened to her."

May stares at her teacup. "We all thought she'd drowned. It was the obvious thing to think. We spread out along the lake, searching under all the docks and in the weeds and lily pads along the shore. And the police dragged the lake. Not a sign of her."

"Someone must have seen Grandpa go to Marmot Lake," insists Van.

"No one came forward." May's voice falters. "The police asked him so many questions. They wouldn't leave him alone. There was a lot of pressure on them to make an arrest, but they had no actual evidence. And then they came back. Twenty-five years later. They hounded him again."

May sounds exhausted. This must be agony for her, I think, resurrecting these memories. I know how hard it can be to think about the past.

"So it all came down to what Esta said," says Van roughly. "She *never* saw Livia in Grandpa's truck. She lied. She must have. Why?"

We sit quietly for a minute.

Then May says, "When it was all over, we decided to stay in the area. It was our home, and no one should be allowed to take that away. We raised your father here. Martin was a joy to us. Oh, we had lots of good times, but Heb never got over the shame. It made him what he is: a bit of a recluse. He didn't want his grandchildren to know, and we won't tell your sisters;

there's no need. Bless him, he forgets the past most days now. Old age isn't all bad. It's given him some peace." May closes her eyes and says, "This is a lot of talk, enough for today. I think I'll have a little rest."

Van reaches out and squeezes her hand. "Thank you, Grandma," he says.

We leave May to her memories. I feel restless and uneasy.

One burning question remains.

What happened to Livia?

❦

That night I decide to go back to the old cabin at the end of the road. The sun has slipped below the ridge and the shadows are long. The mosquitoes are out in droves. But there's something I want to check.

It's dim inside the cabin but still light enough to see what I have come for. I study the letters gouged into the wooden doorway. I trace the *S* and the *T* and then I make out the shape of the first letter, sunken into the wood. *E.*

I say the name out loud. "Esta."

Twelve

It turns out that I haven't scarred Renegade for life after all. The last two mornings I've put his grain bucket in the round pen and left the gate open, and both evenings when I went back, the bucket was empty.

I'm sitting on a stool in the sunshine, rubbing saddle soap into a bridle, enjoying the way the leather turns a rich dark brown. I have one eye on Renegade, but I'm trying not to let him notice. He's sticking his head sideways through the wooden rails of the corral, awkwardly tearing up pieces of grass within his reach. He gives up after a while and wanders into the metal round pen, checking out his empty bucket, which has been lying there since this morning. He grabs the rim with his teeth and flips the bucket back and forth.

I put the bridle down and approach him quietly, climbing over the corral fence so I'm close to the round pen. I slip inside and shut the metal gate. Renegade looks up. He's on the far side, opposite me, the bucket hanging from his mouth in a comical way.

I've left the rope hanging over a rail, ready for this moment. I pick it up and move to the middle of the pen, watching Renegade. He drops the bucket. Tension ripples through his back. He looks poised for flight.

I've been reading how *less* pressure is better. I threw the rope too hard last time. Slowly I raise my arm with the rope. That's all I do. Renegade breaks into a canter. He catches the bucket under his back feet. He kicks out and it skitters into the middle of the pen.

I think about the words I wrote. *Control movement.*

I raise my arm again and Renegade increases his speed. But not crazy-like. Steady. A grin spreads across my face.

He makes three or four circles. His ears are slanted back and his tail swishes from side to side, signs that he is not at all sure about this. He's looking to the outside of the pen as if he wants to be anywhere but here with me. His feet start to slow and I send him on faster again, this time tossing the end of the rope gently onto the ground behind him.

I am the lead mare.

Now. *Change direction.*

I step toward Renegade. That's when things start to go wrong. He swerves toward me, his ears flattened. I leap out of the way. He bucks twice, churning up clods of dirt, and then canters back out to the rails.

I take a few deep breaths. Renegade circles the pen two more times. Sweat breaks out on his flanks.

"Change direction," I mutter. I step toward him again. He speeds up from a canter to a gallop, kicking out sideways as he streaks past. I swear I can feel the wind from his hooves on my face. My legs shake.

"If you want to make him turn," says a voice quietly, "you need to focus on his head and shoulder."

For the first time, I notice Marion Wilson standing outside the round pen.

"Move toward his shoulder," she says. "Hold up your arm. Make a barrier."

I think I get it. Renegade has dropped back to a canter. As he approaches, I take a step toward his shoulder, my arm nearest his nose raised. Renegade tucks his back legs under and skids to a halt. He spins toward the rail and turns, gives a tremendous buck and canters off in the opposite direction.

I glance at Marion triumphantly. She smiles, then says, "Ask for some more turns. Keep his mind on you."

It's easier the next time, and the next. Renegade's turns become smoother. Back and forth. He's breathing hard now.

Then he turns without my asking him to. Marion says, "If he does that again, slap your rope. Tell him no. Tell him he's made a mistake. He can only turn when you say so."

Renegade canters once around the pen and then braces his back legs and starts to turn. I bang the coiled rope against my leg and shout, "No!" Renegade spins around, back in the direction he was going.

"That's good," says Marion. "Now, ask him to turn."

I ask. He turns.

Change direction. It's working! I don't want to stop, but Marion says, "He's had enough."

I know what she means—take away the pressure. I move my eyes away from him and let my shoulders go soft. I turn my back on him.

There is silence behind me except for the sound of Renegade breathing. I peek at him. He's standing still, his head turned away from me, his flanks going in and out.

"Well done," says Marion. I'm not sure if she's talking to Renegade or to me. I feel suddenly ashamed of the way he looks, his coat scruffy, his mane unbrushed, and I say defensively, "He won't let me touch him."

"He will soon," says Marion.

We walk back to the barn together, leaving the round pen gate open. I'm bubbling over with what has just happened. "Thank you for your help," I say finally.

"It just takes a bit to get the hang of it," says Marion. "You'll want to practice that. Pick places along the rails and make him turn exactly where you want him to. And there's no need to tire him out. Less is more."

Marion waits while I put away the tack and the tin of saddle soap. "I actually came to tell you that Tully has iced tea and homemade cookies on the porch for everyone," she says. "He said I would find you out here. He's probably wondering what's happened to us."

I'm more than ready for iced tea. I wipe my dusty hands on my jeans. "Marion," I say as we walk to the lodge, "please don't tell Dad. I don't want him to know yet."

"I'm good at keeping secrets," says Marion.

❧

I practically live at the barn for the next few days. I try to ignore the fact that Van hasn't come around.

Maybe he's still upset about his grandfather. Maybe he blames me. Or maybe he's just hanging out with his youth-group friends. I tell myself I don't care.

I practice with Renegade in the mornings before it gets too hot. He follows a bucket of grain quite willingly into the round pen; maybe he doesn't hate me after all. On the third day, something different happens. Instead of turning his butt to me when he changes direction, he turns into the circle, toward me. His ears flick back and forth and he lowers his head.

I'm sure that this means something, but I'm not sure what.

❧

I'm lying on our dock later in the day, thinking about Renegade, when I see Marion coming across the lake in the blue boat. She goes out in the boat every day, sometimes for hours. I don't have the faintest idea where she goes. She must have explored the whole lake by now. I can't imagine coming on a holiday like this by yourself, and I wonder if she's lonely. At dinner we talk about ordinary things like school or how the cabin renovations are going. Sometimes Tully tells more stories about his travels. Marion's never said anything about having any family.

I walk over to her cabin to meet her. She bumps the boat up against the dock, gathers up her lunch bag and hat and climbs out. Her movements are slow, and I'm shocked by how tired she looks. There are dark smudges under her eyes, and her face looks caved in; that's the only way I can think of to describe it. She ties the boat to a tire on the side of the dock, lowers herself into a deck chair and motions me to sit beside her.

She brightens when I tell her how Renegade makes his turns inward now, looking at me instead of pushing his butt in my face. "That's a great sign, Thea," she says. "He's showing you more respect. He's focusing on you. I'll come out and watch you tomorrow, shall I?"

"That'd be great," I say.

There's something else I want to show her, something I tried at the very end with Renegade. Something I haven't told her about. I want it to be a surprise.

*

Renegade is standing quietly in the round pen, gazing out through the metal rails as usual. I've just put him through his paces. His turns were smooth and consistently to the inside. Now he's resting.

I make a kissing sound. He bends his neck and stares at me. Then he looks away.

I make the kissing sound again. He turns, and this time he makes steady eye contact. He holds it for two, three seconds. Then looks away.

Next time, he holds the eye contact for longer, at least ten seconds. I feel like we are looking right inside each other. The back of my neck prickles.

Then Renegade takes two steps and turns his whole body to face me.

I move sideways a few feet. Renegade moves his head first and then his feet, keeping up with me. I let my breath out. Marion is smiling broadly and she says, "That's marvelous progress, Thea. Marvelous."

Her praise makes me feel warm inside.

But the person I really want to show is Dad.

Thirteen

Tully has unearthed a box of photographs of the ranch. They look like the ones in the old guest books: grainy black-and-whites. Tully says they were taken with a Polaroid camera, the kind where you take the film out of the camera and watch it develop. He thinks they're probably fifty or sixty years old.

We're all looking at them: Tully, Dad, Marion and me. There are pictures of people piled into a hay wagon, riding horses, sitting in boats, playing horseshoes. There's one of a tall woman wearing an apron, and I wonder if it might be a much younger May.

We're passing the photographs around in a circle. Marion is quiet. She takes a long time with each photo, staring intently, as if she were searching for something, and a stack builds up on the arm of her chair.

I come to an abrupt stop when I get to a photograph of a little girl sitting on a pony. A man is holding the lead rope. I recognize them right away. Goose bumps prickle the back of my neck. I feel like I've seen a ghost. "That's Livia Willard," I say. "And her father."

"Who?" says Tully.

I tell them the story of Livia, how I found the newspaper article in the old guest book and how Van and I went to the museum. I leave out the part about Van's grandfather and talking to May. I'm not sure Van would like everyone to know that.

"That's sad," says Dad. "I wonder if she drowned."

"They searched the lake," I say. "They didn't find anything."

"Then someone must have abducted her." Tully is distressed. "To think that it happened here. The poor child. It's horrible."

Marion says nothing, but I know she's listening. Her hands, holding a photograph on her lap, don't move.

Now she gets up and murmurs something about looking at the rest of the photographs another day. Her face is pale, and I think again that she doesn't look well.

She's not. She has a headache, a migraine, she tells us. She's going to turn in early.

⁂

After Marion leaves, my cell phone vibrates. It's Van, texting me.

"Can I go to a party with Van on Friday?" I ask Dad.

"Where?" says Dad.

"A girl called Lindsay's." Dad's frowning slightly and I add, "She's in the church youth group and she lives on a ranch somewhere near here. Van's dad said he'd drive us and pick us up."

"What time will you be back?"

"He'll pick us up at eleven."

"Is someone supervising?"

"Lindsay's parents." I don't know if that's true, but I say it anyway.

I'm not that good at parties, and I usually avoid them, but suddenly it's the most important thing in the world to me that I'm allowed to go.

"Okay," says Dad finally.

I text Van back the good news. I feel all zingy inside, like I want to dance.

❦

Renegade won't do anything right today. His feet are firmly planted and he's not budging. I have to throw the rope hard, letting the end slap his legs, and that makes him buck. He bucks the entire way around the pen.

He's sulking now, staring through the rails as if he's plotting his escape.

I make the kissing sound.

He ignores me.

I'm hot and dusty, and at this very moment I hate horse training. I feel totally fed up with Renegade. Something tells me to stop before I do something I might regret.

Renegade raises his tail and lets loose a steaming pile of manure.

I can't help but laugh. "You win," I say, "but just for today."

Fourteen

On the night of the party, Van's dad drops us off in the driveway of a large log house. Van rings the doorbell and a girl that I recognize from school opens the door.

"Hey, Lindsay," says Van. "This is Thea."

"Hi," says Lindsay. She has long blond hair and she's gorgeous. "It's about time you got here. Come on in. Everyone's downstairs."

Van knows the way. I follow him down a narrow staircase. About twenty kids are sitting around a big room in chairs and on the floor, talking and laughing. There's a Ping Pong table at one end and a large-screen TV. Boxes of pizza, bowls of potato chips and a huge plate of veggies and dip are set out on a table.

Van introduces me around. There's no way I can remember all these names. For a few seconds, everyone stares at me. My smile feels wooden and now I regret coming. They're probably all good friends. I feel like such an outsider.

Van gets a slice of pizza, but I can't eat a thing so I just grab a can of Sprite out of a cooler. I'm mad at myself for feeling so nervous, but I can't help it. I have no idea what to expect. These kids are supposed to be religious. What am I doing here?

The chairs are all taken, so Van and I sit on the floor, our backs against the wall.

Van gets into a long conversation about boats with a boy with blond dreadlocks. I sip my soda and pretend to be interested. To be honest, I'm a little surprised. I haven't been to a lot of parties, but this seems pretty normal. I'm not sure what I was expecting: hymns and prayers?

Someone calls Van over for a game of Ping Pong and he says, "Is that okay?"

"Sure," I say. "I'm fine."

The conversation floats around me but I can't think of a way to make myself part of it. Everyone's talking about the usual stuff: computers, movies, music, parties, summer plans. I'm starting to feel stupid, sitting there not saying anything. I glance over at Van. He's teamed up at the Ping Pong table with a short boy with red hair who I remember is called Mike. At the other end are Lindsay and another girl. They're all laughing and shouting a lot. Van high-fives Mike when they win a game.

I get up, put my empty can of Sprite on a table and head for a door in the corner of the room. I'm pretty sure that no one even notices that I'm leaving.

I slip outside into the backyard. There's a full moon so it's almost as bright as day. I take in a deep breath of the cool night air. Then I notice that I'm not alone. A girl is sitting on the step. She has dark brown hair, streaked with red and cut in feathery layers around her face. There is a ring in her lower lip. She's smoking a cigarette.

Dad used to smoke a pack a day. I hated it—the way it made his clothes smell, the way his fingers turned yellow. Not to mention that I was scared to death that he might get cancer. I guess something shows on my face because the girl waves her cigarette and says, "Sorry."

I shrug. "It's a free world." I figure I need to offer some explanation as to why I'm out here, other than to spy on her. "I just felt like a bit of fresh air," I mumble.

The girl looks at her cigarette and we both giggle. "I'm Chloe," she says.

"I'm Thea."

"I know," says Chloe. She makes a sweeping gesture with her hand. "Sit down."

I sit down on the step beside her.

"You came with Van," she says.

"That's right."

"Are you guys going out?"

"No," I say quickly. "He's just a friend."

"Hmmm." Chloe gives me an appraising look, and I feel my cheeks flush. "He's available, you know."

"What's that supposed to mean?"

"He and Lindsay broke up a couple of months ago."

Van went out with Lindsay. I try to arrange my face so nothing shows, but I'm not sure how I feel about this. Lindsay is so pretty, and she seems really popular.

"We're just friends," I repeat.

Chloe takes a final drag on her cigarette and then drops it on the ground and puts it out with the toe of her runner. She picks up the butt and lays it carefully on the step beside her. "I don't smoke nearly as much as I used to," she says. "But you know—it's a party." She smiles at me, her teeth white against her olive skin. "Van says you're into horses."

Van has been talking about me?

"I used to ride all the time," I say. "I kind of grew up with horses."

"Me too," says Chloe. "I ride almost every day. Do you have a horse now?"

"No. Well, I'm sort of borrowing one."

"Like a lease, you mean?"

"Not exactly." I find myself telling her about Renegade. I tell her about how I'm working him in the round pen and how he's starting to make eye contact with me. I talk more than I mean to, and I cut it off abruptly, embarrassed. Chloe will think I'm a motormouth.

But she looks fascinated. "I'd love to see him," she says. "Maybe I could ride my horse over one day." Now it's Chloe's turn to look embarrassed. "Not that I'm pushy or anything," she says.

"No, I'd love that," I say. "You can come anytime."

Van comes outside then, the screen door banging behind him. "There you are," he says. "I've been looking everywhere for you. You're on for Ping Pong." He smiles at Chloe. "Hey, Chloe," he says.

"Hey," says Chloe. She puts up both her hands. "No cigarette."

"We're trying to get her to quit," says Van.

"Yes, Mother," says Chloe. "Wait a sec," she says to me. "Phone number?" We exchange numbers and enter them into our cell phones. Then she gives me a little nudge with her foot and I get up. I glance back at her as Van and I go inside and she mouths "He likes you" at me.

She grins. She has a great smile. It's contagious. I grin back.

❧

I get caught up in the Ping Pong game. When I make an especially fantastic spike, everyone hollers and I hear myself hollering too. Then someone puts on a movie and Van and I squish onto one end of a long couch. I don't get a chance to talk to Chloe again, though she catches my eye once across the room and smiles. Later, when I look around for her, I can't see her anywhere, and I figure she must have left.

Van's dad picks us up at eleven. I thank Lindsay and her mom, who's sitting upstairs in the living room, looking like she wishes everyone would leave. I fall asleep in the truck, and the next thing I know we're at the Double R and Van's shaking my shoulder.

"See you," he says as I climb out.

"See you," I say.

❧

I can't sleep. How can I be so dead tired one minute and so wide-awake the next? I toss and turn for an hour. My phone hums. There's a text message from Chloe, just saying hi. She can't sleep either. I text her back. Then I lie there and think about Van for a while and wonder how he's feeling about his grandfather. We didn't get a chance to talk about it tonight. There were always too many people around.

Finally I get up and get dressed again in my jeans and a T-shirt. I pull on my running shoes. I close the door quietly behind me and stand on the porch for a moment. It's still bright outside. Moonlight shimmers in a silvery path down the middle of the black lake. A bat flits silently past my head. I hurry to the barn.

It's like we're doing some kind of dance. Just me and Renegade. He moves when I move, shifting his position so he's always facing me. His ears are forward. His eyes are dark and soft in the moonlight.

I feel like an invisible rope connects us. If I back up, he steps toward me. If I turn to the side, he steps with me.

He is watching, always watching.

I turn my back to him and walk across the round pen. I hear his hooves on the ground, following.

He'll learn, Marion told me, *that next to you is the place he wants to be.*

She didn't tell me how I would feel when it happened.

I turn around. Renegade stops, his eyes meeting mine. I make the kissing sound and he takes a step forward.

I kiss again.

Another step. He is so close I can touch him now.

So I do.

I rub him gently between his eyes.

A shiver ripples under his skin, down his neck and along his flanks.

But he doesn't leave.

Fifteen

Dad is awake when I get back to the cabin. He's making hot chocolate in our little kitchen. He doesn't ask me where I've been, but his eyes rake over me. I'm conscious of bits of hay clinging to my running shoes and Renegade's scent in my clothes. I'm bursting with joy over what just happened between Renegade and me. More than anything, I want to tell Dad.

The words stick in my throat. Suddenly, for some stupid reason, my thoughts get mixed up with Mom and I imagine telling her too.

Mom, who I try so hard not to think about. Mom, who loved horses like I do. Mom, who wrecked everything when she left.

I swallow. It's so long since Dad and I have talked about anything that matters. Anything at all. I'm not sure I know how anymore.

"Want some hot chocolate?" he says.

"No thanks," I say.

I feel frozen to the floor. The clock on the wall is ticking loudly. It's half past four. We're both up in the middle of the night. There should be so much to say.

I want Dad to ask me. I want him to say, "Where have you been? What happened?"

But he doesn't. Instead he says, "We're not staying, remember. Not past the fall."

This is Dad's way of telling me that he knows about Renegade. That he doesn't want me to get emotionally attached. It's too late. Sudden tears sting my eyes. For one overwhelming second, I hate Dad. Really hate him.

"I just don't want you to be disappointed," he adds.

Thanks. I get it. I stare past Dad, stone-faced.

He goes back to his bedroom and closes the door.

I put my hands up to my cheeks and breathe in the smell of Renegade. I've just had the best night I can ever remember. Why do I feel so miserable?

⚮

The next day I tackle the snarls in Renegade's mane. I dig my fingers into the middle of the mats, yanking the coarse hairs apart. I use a pair of scissors to snip away the worst knots. I think about getting the bottle of mane detangler from the barn but it's probably old and dried up. I make a mental note to go back to the tack shop and buy some horse shampoo and conditioner.

Marion was here earlier, admiring Renegade. I showed her how he has suddenly accepted my touch. I can run my hands over his whole body—his legs, under his belly, even his ears. We made plans for what comes next.

Renegade stands patiently, his tail switching at a few flies. I've worked through about half of the mane and my fingers are starting to ache. The back of my T-shirt is damp with sweat. Pull, tug. I whisper apologies to Renegade, but his eyes are half closed and his head hangs down.

The comb catches and a plastic tooth breaks. I step back, take a breath. A sudden mental picture catches me off guard. Mom beside me, her long brown fingers skillfully braiding strands of Monty's mane and securing them with tiny black elastics. My clumsy efforts and then Mom's hands on top of mine, gently guiding.

Did that even happen? I've pushed away the memories for so long, I don't know what's real anymore. I swallow a lump that's squeezing my throat.

Concentrate on Renegade. I survey him critically. His coat isn't exactly gleaming. I know it will take days of brushing to get rid of all the dirt and bring out the shine. But he looks much better than he did.

A film of dirt sticks to my arms and my hair and my clothes. My hands are dark with grime. Half an hour more, I tell myself, and then I'll quit for today.

The thought of jumping into the cool lake is tantalizing.

Sixteen

Van comes over after lunch and we go out in his boat. He cuts the motor and we drift in the sun. We talk about the party for a while.

"Chloe likes you," he says. "She has a pretty lousy life. She could probably use another friend."

"What's wrong with her life?" I ask.

"Her dad left a couple of years ago. She's living with her mom and her mom's boyfriend, who she can't stand. I've met him. He's a total jerk."

"What does he do?"

Van shrugs. "He's just a jerk. He hassles her over dumb stuff. And he drinks all the time."

"That sounds depressing." I think about Chloe's infectious grin. She's pretty good at hiding things too.

"What about Chloe's mom? Does she stick up for her?"

"Her mom doesn't care what Chloe does as long as she stays out of the way. She doesn't even care that Chloe smokes."

My dad would freak if he caught me with a cigarette. And he asked a million questions before he let me go to the party. Something shifts inside me. Slightly. Maybe my life isn't so bad.

"Chloe spends most of her time riding. If she didn't have her horse, I don't know how she'd survive," says Van.

"She's going to ride over to my place sometime," I say.

"That's great," says Van. He sounds like he really means it, and I wonder if all the youth-group kids care about each other that much.

I lift my hot hair off my shoulders and twist it into a braid. I think about going swimming. Van's been leaning back, his baseball cap tipped over his eyes, but now he sits up. Turns out he's thinking about swimming too. "There's a good spot to land on Spooky Island," he says.

It only takes a few minutes to get to the island. Van turns the motor off and lifts the propeller out of the water; then he guides the boat between two fallen trees that stick out from the shore. He ties the boat to a branch and we climb out, wading across smooth slippery rocks until we get to the shore.

The island is small and covered with scraggly dead trees. Dry sticks are scattered all over the ground; they're sharp under our bare feet so we have to step carefully. Van shows me a fort he worked on for years. He pretends to be offended when I tell him it looks like a random pile of branches. He digs into the middle of it and produces a grimy jar with a rusty lid. "I used to leave messages in here," he says with a grin.

Van strips off his shirt. I've got my bathing suit on under my clothes but I still feel shy taking off my shirt and shorts. We wade in from a grassy bank to swim. The weeds feel like ropes around my legs until we get to deeper water. I float on my back and stare up at the sky. One puffy white cloud is floating in a sea of blue.

I feel perfect right now. If only I could save this feeling for when we have to move again.

❧

On the way back, we talk about Van's grandfather and Livia Willard. I've been waiting for Van to bring it up and he does, finally. He says he can't stop thinking about it, wishing there was some way he could change the past.

I know all about wanting to change the past. It doesn't work. I could have told Van that.

"Grandpa's gotta be the gentlest guy in the universe," says Van. "He's had to live with this for so long. It's not fair. And what I really hate is there's nothing I can do about it."

A cold pit opens up in my stomach. Van is convinced that his grandfather is innocent. Could he be wrong? Then I think of that sweet old man with his birds, and none of it makes sense.

"Someone out there must know something," I say. "A little girl can't just disappear like that."

"Yeah, well she did."

"It must have been hard on your grandmother too," I say.

"Yeah," says Van. "But she's tougher than Grandpa. She's kind of a rock. She's always there for everyone. Always."

Van is quiet for a few minutes, brooding.

I say, "How did the chess game go?"

"Oh that," says Van with a sigh. "Grandpa checkmated me in eight moves. It made his day."

⁂

We cut across the lake and slowly follow the forested shoreline back to the ranch. Van says if we're lucky we might spot some wildlife—a bear or a moose. The boat noses around a point and we're at the edge of the marshy bay in front of the old abandoned cabin. Two black ducks with white patches on their heads skitter through the lily pads. They take off into the sky with a racket.

Van turns the motor off, and we drift.

"I wonder if that old boat is worth salvaging," says Van.

A boat is pulled up on the bank, half hidden in bushes. Faded red paint is peeling along the sides, and a fist-sized hole gapes near the back. It doesn't look like anything I'd want to ride in.

"Be my guest," I say. I study the cabin. It's not possible, but I'd swear it's sunk even deeper into the weeds today. Sun glints off the windows and turns the moss on the shingles a fluorescent green. Everything looks utterly neglected. It's hard to imagine Esta and Iris playing here so long ago.

And then I catch a shadow of movement behind a pane of grimy glass. I suck in my breath.

For a second a face peers out, wavy through the dust, as though underwater. It fades back into darkness.

"There's someone in the cabin," I say softly.

"What?" says Van.

"Behind the window. Someone was looking at us."

"I don't see anyone." Van sounds skeptical.

I lean forward, my eyes riveted on the window. Nothing.

"There *was* someone there," I say slowly. "I'm sure of it."

We wait for a few minutes, watching. Two squirrels chase each other down a tree, chattering shrilly and making me jump. Then it's dead quiet again. I imagine a shadowy figure standing back from the window, staying perfectly still, waiting for us to leave.

"It looks pretty deserted to me," says Van. "You want to check it out?"

There's nowhere that looks like a good landing place for the boat. And I'm not so sure I want to go inside the cabin anyway. I sigh. "No, I guess not."

Van starts the motor. He skirts the lily pads and points the boat back to deeper water. I look over my shoulder.

I don't really care whether Van believes me or not. There was someone there. I *know* it. I frown, trying to bring into focus the fleeting image of the face in the window.

I'm almost positive it was Marion Wilson.

Seventeen

The next morning, Renegade and I are standing in the middle of the round pen. His ears flick back and forth as if he's thinking *Now what?* He lowers his head and sniffs the saddle blanket and saddle that rest on the ground beside us.

I coil my rope and rub it over his legs and up over his neck and ears. I bounce it up and down on his back. He's used to this. He turns his head and looks at me, his eyes soft. *We've done this before,* he says. *Get on with it.*

He pays a little more attention when I pick up the saddle blanket. His head raises and he takes a step backward. I go with him, holding the blanket in my arms. He stretches out his neck, blows through his nostrils. Slowly I feel him relax.

I lay the blanket over his back and then take it off before he has a chance to get upset. I do this several times. Finally I leave the blanket there. All the time, I'm alert to the signals Renegade is giving me. He's lowered his head again, and his mouth is gently chewing. All good signs.

I flap the sides of the blanket and thump it up and down. I slide it up his neck, almost to his ears, and back down again.

No problem.

I eye the saddle lying on the ground by my feet. A tickle of uneasiness curls in my stomach. I slide the right stirrup over the saddle horn, lay the cinch and the latigo over the seat. I pick the saddle up.

That's when Renegade bolts.

I make a loud *shooshing* sound as he pivots away. I want him to think that it's my idea that he go, not his. I put the saddle down and drive him around the pen with the rope, one lap, then two. A turn to the left. A turn to the right.

I allow Renegade to slow his steps and stop. I make the kissing sound and he walks toward me. His ears are forward, his lips move. He stands quietly.

Before I can change my mind, I pick up the saddle again, take a deep breath and place it on his back. Not a muscle twitches as I walk around him and lower the stirrup and latigo.

Back to his left side. I reach under his belly for the latigo. My hands are shaking. I'm not sure what's going to happen. I've been practicing in the barn, the saddle resting on a sawhorse. I tighten the latigo firmly and make a knot.

I stand back.

Renegade plunges forward. He crow-hops across the pen and bucks hard. Again and again. He's making a frantic effort to get the strange thing off his back. My heart thuds as saddle strings whip around and stirrups slap his sides. Dirt flies.

I'm starting to freak out, and then Renegade loses interest. Just like that. He stands still. I can almost see him thinking *Is this worth it?* I kiss and he comes to me willingly. I stroke his face and his ears.

"Next time," I say, "I'm going to ride you."

❧

I go straight to Tully's computer and search for sites on horse training. Earlier Marion had suggested I type in *natural horsemanship* and *horse whisperer*. One link leads to another. I find lots more good stuff to add to what I've already got. But when I try to use the printer, it whirrs and hums and then makes a sick noise.

Then silence.

I investigate the problem. A sheet of paper is caught in the rollers. I fiddle for ten minutes before I get it out. It's deeply creased across the middle and I've torn the corner off, but you can still read it. The title at the top says *Anaphylactic Shock and Wasp Stings*.

I'm about to crumple it up and throw it in the wastepaper basket when I hesitate. Someone wanted it badly enough to print it.

Tully comes in from outside. He looks over my shoulder. I hold up the paper. "Is this yours?" I ask. "It's something about wasp stings."

"Not mine," says Tully. "It must be Marion's. She was using the computer a little while ago. Said she'd jammed the printer. I was just coming in to have a look at it."

"I've fixed it," I say.

Why would Marion be worried about wasps? I haven't seen any around here. And what is ana—*whatever*—shock?

I read the first few sentences.

Anaphylactic shock is a severe allergic reaction that can be life threatening. On rare occasions complete respiratory failure and death can occur within seconds to minutes of exposure to the trigger. Common triggers are high-protein foods, such as shellfish and peanuts, and the venom of stinging insects, such as bumblebees and yellow jacket wasps.

Sounds lovely. I push the paper aside and sink back into the world of horses.

※

In the afternoon I help Tully clean the lodge. Dad's working, Marion is out in the boat and Tully has chased the dogs outside, so we're by ourselves. Classical music is blaring. I can hear it even over the roar of the vacuum cleaner. Beethoven, Tully tells me, but that means nothing to me. Though I have to admit I like it more than I thought I would.

I'm dusting, and every once in a while Tully turns the vacuum off to tell me a story about the object I'm dusting: a piece of pottery from Peru, a carved wooden elephant from India, a Venetian mask, a chess set with detailed figures shaped like pirates and British soldiers. It takes ten times as long to get the cleaning done, but I like Tully's stories and I'm in no hurry.

When we're finished, Tully asks me to take some freshly laundered towels to Marion's cabin; after that I'm free, he says. The towels are stacked on top of the dryer. I pick out a bath towel, a couple of hand towels and a facecloth and head outside.

The blue boat is gone and nobody answers my knock on the door of cabin three. I glance out at the lake, but there's no sign of Marion. The water is slate gray and a breeze ruffles the surface. The sky has clouded over and it looks like it might rain.

I knock again but no one answers. The door is unlocked, so I go inside. It's the first time I've been in here since Marion came. The cabin is much smaller than ours. It has one main room with a kitchen sink, gas stove and mini-fridge at the end. There's one bedroom and a tiny bathroom. Everything is so neat. You'd hardly know anyone was staying here, except for the book sitting on the table beside the armchair and a jacket hanging on a hook by the door.

I take the towels into the bathroom and set them down on the counter. It's just as tidy in here. A toothbrush and a tube of toothpaste with one of those clip things on it sit in a drinking glass, a damp facecloth is folded over the edge of the sink, and the used towels are in the tub. I gather them up.

As I leave the cabin, something on the table beside the couch catches my eye. It's a beautiful carved box—the only personal thing of Marion's I've seen. It's made of golden wood and has a piece of abalone shell embedded in the lid. It reminds me of something that Tully might have brought back from one of his trips.

I put the towels down and touch the abalone. It's smooth, like silk. Curious, I pick up the box and lift the lid. Inside the box, a chain with a heart-shaped gold locket rests on a piece of white cloth. In the middle of the heart, a name is engraved in scrolly letters:

Livia

Eighteen

The thrum of a boat engine jerks me out of my state of shock. Quickly I close the lid and put the box down.

I grab the used towels, hurry out the front door of the cabin and wave at Marion, who's almost back at the dock. "Clean towels," I holler as I scurry up the path to the road.

I can't talk to Marion right now.

I need to think.

I go back to our cabin and lie down on my bed. My head whirls. There can't be more than one Livia. It's just too big a coincidence.

I need to make some sense out of this. I get up and search for a piece of paper and a pen. I sit at the table and make a list of everything I know about Marion.

1. *comes all the way from England*
2. *goes out in the boat every day—where?*
3. *possibly lied about friends being here ten years ago*
4. *what was she doing in the old abandoned cabin?*
5. *acted weird when we looked at old photographs*
6. *wasp stings?*
7. *gold locket with Livia's name*

I stare at my list for a long time. At the bottom I write:

Who is Marion Wilson?

I fold the paper in half and put it in my pocket. I need to talk to Van.

❧

It's the first time I've taken one of the ranch boats to Van's place by myself. The wind blows in my face the whole way and the boat struggles against the tiny waves that break against the bow. I'm worried that I'll never get there.

Van meets me at the dock. I had told him over the phone about the gold locket, and he's excited. "Grandma's in the garden," he says.

We find her kneeling on a foam mat, thinning carrots. She straightens her back when she sees us and says, "Hello, Thea."

"Hi," I say.

The first few drops of rain start to fall, spattering on the frilly green leaves of a mound of lettuce. May stands up stiffly. "I only do a couple of rows at a time. It keeps my hands in the dirt and that's what I like."

"Grandma," says Van, "we want to ask you a few questions."

"About that business with Livia Willard?" she says sharply, and I wonder how she guessed.

I nod my head.

"It's best to let sleeping dogs lie," says May.

"This could be important," says Van.

May is silent for a moment. Finally she says, "All right, for a few minutes."

We run to the house in the rain. May washes her hands at the kitchen sink. She takes a jug of lemonade out of the fridge and puts it on a round wooden table, along with three glasses. "Sit down," she says.

We sit. "The family's gone to town and Heb is asleep," says May. She gives me a long steady gaze. "What is it you want to know, Thea?"

I swallow. I'm not sure where to begin. So I plunge right in. "This might be hard to remember, but did Livia have a gold necklace? A little heart with her name on it?"

May is still for a moment, and I imagine her reaching back into the past. She pours lemonade into the glasses. Her back is straight, her movements slow. Then she folds her strong brown hands together and says, "How did you know?"

I hesitate. I don't want May to think I was snooping. I wasn't. It was just that the box was so beautiful. So I tell her about the locket in Marion's box.

"That's extraordinary," says May slowly. "I don't understand it."

"So Livia *did* have a necklace like that?" says Van.

"I haven't thought of it for years," says May. "It was a ridiculous thing for a little girl to have. Her father gave it to her. Livia was very proud that her name was on it. She came running to the kitchen to show me when they arrived that year. Esta and Iris never owned anything so pretty."

"It doesn't make sense," says Van. "Why does Marion Wilson have Livia's necklace?"

"Was Livia wearing the necklace when she disappeared?" I say.

"I can't be certain," says May, "but I think so. She never took it off, even when she went in the water."

"There's something else," I say. "This is going to sound crazy, but do you remember anything about wasps that year?"

"Wasps?" May sounds uncertain. "No, nothing about wasps."

"What do wasps have to do with this?" says Van.

I tell them about the paper Marion left in the printer.

A door shuts somewhere in the house. May says quickly, "Heb is awake. I don't want him to hear any of this." She reaches out and holds my hand. Her hand is steady, not shaking like mine. "Thea, you must tell me anything you find out," she says quietly.

"I will," I promise.

❧

Van phones me late that night. I'm in bed, almost asleep. I've just talked to Chloe for an hour, mostly about horses. I roll over on my side, my cell phone cradled against my ear.

"The wasps," says Van. "Grandma's remembered."

I'm wide awake now.

"She says there was a huge wasp nest above the door of the old cabin. She remembers that Livia's mother knew about the wasp nest and had told the girls not to play there that summer. Grandma said that when they were searching for Livia, the cabin was one of the places they looked. She said the nest had been knocked down and wasps were swarming around."

My spine prickles. "That printout of Marion's *has* to mean something."

"What did you say it was called—some kind of shock?" says Van.

"Anafa…latic or something like that."

"I've never heard of that before," says Van.

We talk for a while longer, but we don't get anywhere. After we say good night, I lie awake for a long time. I'm convinced that the wasp nest is an important piece of the puzzle, but I have no idea where it fits.

Nineteen

It's been raining hard all day. I brought a book over to the lodge this morning and have been curled up in an armchair most of the morning, reading. Tully is working on the computer in his office, designing a new website for the lodge, and Dad is laying a pine floor in cabin five. There has been no sign of Marion.

I put on a slicker and run out to the barn a few times, once to feed Renegade and the other times just to visit. He's in his shelter, sleepy-eyed, but he nickers when he sees me. In the afternoon there's a break between rain showers, but it doesn't look like it will last. Tully takes the dogs for a walk. I go to our cabin and make myself a grilled cheese sandwich for lunch and then come back to the lodge to use the computer.

I hunt around in a pile of loose papers for the article on wasp stings but it's gone.

I google *wasp stings* and *anaphylactic shock*, making a wild guess at the spelling. Google corrects my spelling, and I click on a few sites. This time I read the articles carefully, searching for clues.

One article calls anaphylactic shock *an explosive overreaction of the body*. It lists the symptoms: painful hives, swollen tongue, difficulty breathing, loss of blood pressure, unconsciousness, death.

I keep reading.

The insect responsible for the largest number of severe allergic reactions is the yellow jacket wasp. Anaphylactic shock is usually caused by multiple stings.

Anaphylactic shock is more likely to occur in people who have asthma.

Although rare, death can occur within as little as five minutes.

Five minutes. I feel slightly sick. I tilt my chair back, thinking.

It's pouring again. The rain is thundering on the metal roof. Tully comes back with the dogs, yelling at them to stay on the porch until they're dry.

I stare at the computer screen. *Asthma.* I frown, reread that part. *Anaphylactic shock is more likely to occur in people who have asthma.* Why does that seem important? My brain is foggy with information. Finally I turn off the computer and take Tully up on his offer to make us some hot chocolate.

While I sip my hot chocolate, I hunt through the old guest book, studying the names of the guests who were at the ranch the same time as the Willards. Is it possible Marion's family stayed at the ranch too, that Marion played with Esta and Iris? Is that how this all fits together? I imagine Marion as a little girl, finding the gold locket that Livia dropped somewhere and keeping it because it was so pretty. I check the names carefully, especially those that look like they were written by a child. But nowhere do I find the name Marion.

Later, when I call Van to tell him what I've learned, he says, "Thea, don't you remember? Grandma told us. *Livia* had asthma."

⚜

Marion doesn't join us for dinner. Tully sends me over to see if she's okay. She comes to the door of her cabin when I knock, wearing a dressing gown and blue slippers. She looks ill.

"It's nothing," she says. "A migraine headache, that's all. But I don't feel like eating."

I don't know how to act around Marion now. I felt like I knew her when we were working with Renegade. Almost like she was a friend. Now I realize that I don't know her at all. "Can I bring you anything?" I say.

"I've got some canned soup. I'll make that later. I'm sorry you've had to come all the way over here in the rain."

Marion wants me to go. I can see it in her eyes, which are glassy and filled with pain.

"If you're sure then," I say.

Marion closes the door, but I have the feeling that she's watching me through the window as I run back to the lodge.

After dinner, I offer to do the dishes while Dad and Tully head over to cabin five in the rain to look at the new floor. The phone rings while I'm loading the dishwasher.

I pick it up on the third ring. "Double R Ranch," I say. "Can I help you?"

A woman answers, her voice crisp. She has an English accent. "I'd like to speak with Marion Wilson, please."

It's the first time anyone has called for Marion. I wonder if I'm speaking to someone in London (the only place I can think of in England), although the connection is so clear the woman could be in the next room. I hesitate. I'm pretty sure this woman is calling long distance, but Marion made it clear that she wanted to be left alone.

"She doesn't want to be disturbed," I say. "She's not feeling well. Maybe I could take a message."

The woman is insistent. "It's important that I talk to her."

"Well…"

"It's about her sister." There is a pause and then she says, "It's about Esta."

Twenty

Of course I get Marion. She takes the call in the office. She has thrown a long red poncho over her dressing gown and she's wearing a pair of gumboots. We've both left pools of water on the floor. Trembling, I wipe them up with an old towel. Marion has shut the office door. I can hear the murmur of her voice, but I can't make out what she is saying.

I am reeling with shock. Esta is not a common name. Except for Esta Willard, I have never heard of anyone called Esta. So for one crazy second, when the woman on the phone said Marion's sister was Esta, I thought that Marion was Livia. I don't believe in ghosts but maybe—*somehow*—Livia miraculously survived whatever it was that happened almost sixty years ago.

I don't really believe that. I believe that Livia is dead. So there is only one other thing that makes sense. Marion must be Iris.

I'm trembling with confusion and something that feels like anger or even betrayal. What is Marion (the name is a lie, but I can't think of her as Iris—not yet) doing here? What does she want?

I'm staring out the window, watching the rain lash the gray lake, my thoughts spinning around in circles, when I hear her put the phone down.

"That was my friend in England," she says, coming out of the office. "It's my sister. She hasn't been well, but she's much worse now. I'll have to go back to England right away."

I turn around. "You mean Esta," I say. "Your sister Esta."

Something flickers through Marion's eyes, almost as if she is afraid.

She knows I know.

My heart starts to race. "You're Iris Willard," I blurt out.

Marion is silent but her face has drained of color. I know I am right.

The back of my neck feels icy. "I don't understand. Why did you lie? Why did you say your name was Marion Wilson?"

When Marion finally speaks, her voice is calm. "I didn't know if there was anyone here who would remember the Willard case. It was so long ago I figured it was unlikely, but I thought it was better to remain anonymous. So I used a different name. And I told my friend Louise—that's the woman who called—that she was to ask for Marion Wilson if she needed to contact me."

"You said you had friends who stayed here ten years ago," I say. "Did you make that up too?"

"I had to give Tully some reason why I wanted to come to the ranch. He was so adamant that he wasn't open for business yet. So, yes, I invented the story of my friends loving it here. I told him that I probably wouldn't be back in Canada again and that this was my only chance to stay here."

Marion presses her fingers against her forehead. She looks gray. "I can't talk about this anymore right now, Thea. My head is splitting. This is going to have to wait until tomorrow."

"Just tell me one thing," I say. "Why *are* you here?"

"I'm looking for Livia," she says simply.

※

Van and I talk on the phone late into the night. Van is excited because he thinks we are closer to clearing his grandfather's name. We go over and over the possible scenarios. It always comes back to one thing: the wasps.

We know that Marion has been looking up anaphylactic shock and wasp stings on the Internet. We know that there was a wasp nest at the old cabin and that something or someone had knocked it down. We know that Esta and Iris used to play there. The fact that they were forbidden to go there that summer means nothing, Van and I agree. Kids always do what they're not supposed to do.

Just suppose Esta had taken Iris and Livia to the cabin that day. Just suppose Livia had been stung…

If Livia died of anaphylactic shock, someone must have known. Someone must have hidden her body. There is only one possible person: Esta. But why did she do it?

And Iris—how much did Iris know?

Twenty-One

Marion (I don't think I will ever be able to call her Iris) looks much older the next day. Her face is gray and her eyes are shadowed with black circles. She finds me with Renegade. I have just fed him, and for a few minutes we lean against the fence and watch him eat.

"I'm leaving this afternoon," she says. "I'm driving back to Vancouver and flying to England tomorrow morning."

"Is it serious? Esta, I mean?" I ask.

"Very. She has cancer. She only has a few weeks left to live. I want to be there with her." Marion turns and looks at the barn. "This isn't the barn that was here when I was a child," she says. "It was much bigger and it had an enormous hay loft. I don't remember much about our holidays here but I do remember the barn. I used to practically live in it. I wonder if they tore it down, or perhaps it burned down."

Marion does something unexpected then. She reaches out and grips my hand. Her fingers are icy. "This isn't easy for me."

"It isn't easy for Heb and May either," I blurt out.

Marion drops my hand. "Heb and May?" She sounds uncertain.

"My friend Van's grandparents. They were working at the ranch when Livia disappeared."

"I remember," says Marion slowly. "May was the cook. We loved her. And her husband Heb. He was wonderful with us kids."

"Esta said that she saw Livia riding in Heb's truck the afternoon she disappeared."

"Yes," says Marion softly. "Yes, that's what she said."

I take a deep breath. "Van and I know about the wasp nest at the old cabin. We think Livia died from wasp stings."

Marion doesn't look surprised. Just tired. "All these years that I've thought about it, I didn't remember going to the cabin that day," she says. "They say you block out memories that are too painful. Maybe that's what I did. Oh, I had a vague picture of a cabin where we used to play. I don't think I liked it, but I didn't like most of the things Esta made me do. I didn't remember going there on the day Livia disappeared. But on Saturday, when I went back to look at the cabin, after all this time, I did remember."

So I *had* seen Marion in the cabin. My heart starts to beat hard. "What did you remember?"

"There was a huge wasp nest over the back door," says Marion slowly. "We had been forbidden to play there that summer because of it. I wonder now if my stepmother was allergic to wasps and was afraid that Livia might be allergic too. Or if she knew how dangerous a wasp sting could be for an asthmatic."

Marion is silent for a moment, her face etched with pain.

Then she says quietly, "I remember Esta throwing the rock."

Marion's words stun me. An icy chill settles over my back and neck. I stare at her in horror.

"Livia was standing under the nest. I was down by the lake. Perhaps I had stood up for myself for once and refused to go in the cabin. I don't know. Maybe Esta told Livia there was a surprise for her inside. This is all conjecture. I don't remember. But for some reason Livia was under the nest—I do remember that—and Esta threw a rock and the nest fell down."

"Livia was stung," I say.

"Many many times, I expect," says Marion. She adds softly, "I'm sure Esta never thought the nest would fall. She might have thought Livia would get stung once. She hated Livia, you see. She was so jealous of her. But I can't believe that she ever wanted her to die."

I don't know what to say. I wish Van were here. A chilly wind is blowing and I hug my arms to my chest. Renegade walks over to the fence, a wisp of hay hanging from his mouth. I stroke his face.

"That's all I can tell you, Thea," says Marion. "I don't know what happened after that. I remember nothing between that and my aunt coming from England. Why didn't I tell anyone what I saw? I don't know. I was so young. And afraid of my sister."

"May says they found you in your cabin, asleep. She says you cried and cried and were hysterical when the police talked to you."

"I expect I was afraid to tell. Maybe I was confused. When I was little, I was so frightened of Esta."

I remember May saying *It's a terrible thing, to be afraid of your own sister.*

The sky, heavy and gray, bursts open all of a sudden, showering us with rain, and we dash for the barn. We stand in the doorway, watching the rain drench the ground, forming puddles almost instantly. Renegade has disappeared inside his shelter.

"There's something that doesn't makes sense," I say. "Why didn't Esta go for help? Why did she just let Livia die?"

"I think Livia probably stopped breathing within minutes. Esta must have panicked. In a sense, she had killed Livia, even though she didn't mean to. Maybe she thought she would be charged with murder. I don't know." Marion sighs. "It all happened such a long, long time ago. In some ways it doesn't matter now."

I think of Heb's and May's suffering and I feel angry again. "If you really believe that, then why are you here?" I say.

"I want to find Livia's body," says Marion. "I want her to have a proper burial."

"But why now? It's been almost sixty years. Why did you come back now? And what if we're wrong? What if Esta had nothing to do with it?"

At first I don't think Marion is going to answer me. And then she says, "Let's go back to my cabin. There's something I'd like to show you."

*

It's Livia's gold necklace. She takes it out of the box and puts it in my hand. My cheeks flush. I can't tell Marion that I've already seen it.

"Where did you get it?" I say.

"I found it a few weeks ago," says Marion. "In Esta's house."

I stare at Marion, trying to figure out what that means.

"I didn't even know Esta was sick," says Marion. "Esta left my aunt and uncle's when she turned eighteen. We never stayed in touch. I wasn't afraid of her anymore but we were never close. I lived with my aunt and uncle even after I grew up. When they died, the training stable became mine. I never married, never wanted a family. I had lots of friends and, of course, my horses. I made a good life for myself. But Esta just disappeared."

"Did you ever see her?"

"Once, in the distance, on a busy street in London. I thought of calling out to her but I didn't. I heard bits from time to time from an old friend of Esta's who still lived in our village. Nothing very good. Esta became an alcoholic and was in and out of rehab clinics for years. And then my friend Louise went to visit a cousin who was in the hospital. Her cousin was sharing a room with a woman who has cancer. A nurse came in and called the woman Esta. Louise knew that I have a sister named Esta and that we're estranged. Because it's an unusual name, she looked at the chart at the end of her bed. It said *Esta Willard*."

Marion takes the locket from my hand. She studies it for a moment and then lays it back in the box. "I went to see Esta in the hospital. She's the only family I have left. I asked her if there was anything I could do. She wanted me to go to her house, a flat in a poorer part of London, and pick up a few things. That's when I found the locket, in the back of a drawer, behind a wooly shawl that Esta had asked me to look for. I knew what it meant right away."

I feel sick. "So Livia *was* wearing the necklace when she disappeared."

Marion nods.

My head reels. "It's proof," I whisper. "It means that Esta was there when Livia died. She must have taken the locket from Livia's body."

"Deep inside I think I always knew it was Esta," says Marion. "I just didn't remember what happened. Until I came back here."

"That's why you've been going out in the boat every day," I say. "To look for Livia. But how…?"

I stare at Marion. I can't imagine how she could possibly think she might find Livia's body now.

"It's not as impossible as it sounds," says Marion. "I have an idea where to look. I told you I don't remember much about our holidays on the ranch, but there is one thing I do remember. It terrified me.

Esta was always out in the boat. She was allowed to go out by herself, and sometimes she made me go with her. She found a cave somewhere on the lake, I don't remember where. She took me there. It wasn't very big. Esta made me go in by myself. She made me stay in there until she said I could come out. I remember being petrified. It was so dark. I kept calling out to see if she was still there, but she didn't answer. I finally crawled out after what seemed like forever. Esta was sitting on a boulder, laughing at me. I've never ever forgotten it."

"Livia—"

"I think Esta took Livia's body to the cave," says Marion. "I've looked and looked for it. I know we had to go in a boat to get there. There was a boat at the old cabin. Esta could have used that."

"Do you remember anything else?" I ask.

"There were red rocks everywhere. Big boulders. Maybe the red color was from iron or something. It's the only clue I have."

I feel myself go still inside.

Van will know.

Twenty-Two

"I've never seen a cave there," says Van. "But it's the only place on the lake with red rocks."

We're in Van's boat, heading across the lake to the secret inlet he took me to before. The rain is slanting like fine needles into the flat gray lake, and it's cold.

Marion sits in the bow, her back very straight, the hood of her raincoat pulled up over her head.

When we get to the bay, Van lifts the propeller out. We trade places and he rows. His hands are red with the cold, and water drips off the brim of his baseball cap. The rain rattles on the lily pads. Van noses the boat through the narrow opening in the cliff wall, into the hidden pool.

Steep banks loom on either side of us and there's a dank smell of wet rotten leaves. It's so dark it feels like evening, but it's only early afternoon. My jacket isn't waterproof and it's plastered to my back. Rain drips down my neck.

"Could this be it?" says Van.

"I don't know," says Marion. "I just don't remember."

We stare up at the slope at the far end. Reddish boulders are strewn across it, some covered with patches of lime green moss.

"The rocks could have moved," says Van. "Like a slide. Enough to cover up the opening of a cave."

There's only one place to land. It's a tiny strip of rocky beach at the bottom of the slope, not much wider than the boat. Van and I get out but Marion stays in the boat. She looks ill, her face like chalk.

Van and I scramble across the boulders, working our way along the bottom of the slope. The boulders are slick in the rain, and I use my hands to try and get a grip.

"I don't know," says Van. He gazes up. "It could have been anywhere."

"I don't think Esta would have been able to carry Livia very far," I say.

Van sighs. "It's hopeless. There's no way we can move any of these rocks."

I don't want to give up, not yet. A gust of wind drives the rain into my eyes. I reach out for the next boulder and my foot slips. I grab onto a mound of moss. It breaks off in my fingers in a sodden clump.

I stare at the expanse of rock underneath, speckled with bits of soil. Something has been scratched into the surface. It looks like the end of a rectangle. My fingernails dig into the moss and I pull back another clump. I brush away the dirt.

Icy needles slide down my back and I start to shiver.

I know what I am looking at now, gouged crudely into the red boulder.

A cross.

***

Van and I come back in the afternoon, when the rain has stopped. Dad, Tully and Van's dad, Martin, follow us in one of the ranch boats. They have crow-bars, shovels and a flashlight. Van's mother, Jane, is at the lodge with Marion, drinking strong hot tea and talking. Heb and May are at home, waiting.

Van and I stand around and watch while the men use the crowbars to try and shift the boulders beside the cross. At first nothing will move. They work for fifteen, twenty minutes, straining with the effort.

Finally a huge boulder comes loose and rolls down into the water, landing with a great splash.

Tully grunts. "There's something behind here. A bit of a space."

My heart is pounding. Martin pries another boulder loose. There's a lot of rubble now, smaller rocks that the men dig out of the way with the shovels.

And then we all see it. The mouth of a small dark cave.

Dad squats down on his knees and peers into the opening. "It's too dark," he says. "I can't see."

Tully gets the flashlight from the boat and passes it to Dad. Dad shines it into the cave. Time seems to stand still for a moment. I can hear water dripping somewhere. I hug my arms to my chest.

Dad's breath goes in sharply. "I see something," he says.

There is a long pause. He stands up. His face is white. "It looks like it could be bones."

Tully, Van and Martin look inside the cave, one by one, silently, but I don't want to.

We have found Livia. I knew when I saw the cross, but it is still a shock.

"I think we should pray," says Martin quietly. We bow our heads.

"Yea, though I walk through the valley of the shadow of death, I will fear no evil: For thou art with me..."

While he speaks, I stare at the cross gouged into the rock. It blurs over with my tears. I can't concentrate on the words. I don't remember anything Martin says afterward, but his steady voice is comforting. When he is finished, we all say, "Amen."

I can't stop shivering. Van takes my freezing hand in his and slips it into his pocket.

Twenty-Three

Tully contacts the police and they come out the next day and retrieve Livia's bones. Marion is still here. She has changed her plans. She'll stay until tomorrow and then she's going to Vancouver, where she is making arrangements to have Livia buried beside her father and mother.

In the afternoon, I take Marion in the boat to Van's place to meet May and Heb. May is waiting for her, watching from the porch.

Marion has tea with May and Heb in their sitting room, surrounded by the beautiful birds. Van and I stay outside, throwing sticks for Prince. When it's time for Marion to leave, May walks down to the boat and hugs her. They are so different:

May big and strong, and Marion like one of Heb's birds. But they are both crying.

❦

For once, Dad and I are eating breakfast together. We're hunched over bowls of cereal. He's usually up way earlier than me, but today he has slept in. Lines of exhaustion crease his face.

"Marion is leaving today," I say. It takes all my courage to say the next part. "I'm going to ride Renegade. Before she goes."

Dad stares at me.

I feel myself falter, but this is the most important thing in the world to me right now. "Will you come and watch?"

He hesitates and then says, "I've got too much work to do."

"Marion says I have a gift with horses," I say desperately. Somehow I think that this might make him hear me. "I told her it was because of you, that you taught me to ride."

Pain flickers through Dad's eyes. "Thea, your mother gave you your gift," he says tersely. "Not me."

What's Dad talking about? I'd had hundreds of lessons from him, usually in a group with four or five other kids who came to our stable. He'd cheered for me at all my horse shows. A memory pushes in—trotting around the show ring on Monty, searching the stands for Mom's face and then spotting her on the sidelines, not watching me at all but talking to a client instead.

"What do you mean?" I say.

"Mom was the one who put you on your first horse. I thought you were too little—you were only four—but she was determined. She spent months walking you on a lead rope. She never got tired of it."

"Dixie," I say slowly. "The horse was called Dixie. She was really a pony, wasn't she?"

"That's right. It took your mother ages to find her. She searched all over the Valley. She said it had to be the perfect pony."

"The photograph of you and me on Skipper," I say. "I thought—"

"Your mother popped you up and took that photo," says Dad. "You and I never moved out of the driveway. You'd been out riding with Mom; you'd just got off Dixie. I didn't take over the lessons until you were six and started going in shows. I taught all the lessons at our stable."

I feel like I have been kicked in the stomach. Memories flood back, memories that must have always been there. Mom, standing in the round pen, circling me around and around on the end of a lunge line.

Mom picking me up when I fell and putting me back on. Mom promising me that one day I would have my own horse to train. How could I have forgotten?

"And Monty," says Dad. "Mom found Monty for you too. Same thing. He had to be perfect. It wasn't that she didn't care about you, Thea. She was just always so tied up with the business side of the stable."

I swallow. I don't trust my voice.

"It's those early years with Mom that gave you your passion for horses," says Dad. "She gave you your gift."

Passion. I know I will hold on to that word, like something precious.

"I didn't know," I say.

"It's your mother you should thank," says Dad.

We push away our bowls of cereal. I guess neither of us is hungry now.

Dad stands up. "I'm sorry," he says, and I think that he means much more than not coming to see me ride Renegade. And then he is gone.

❧

The sun shines down out of a bright blue sky and the air has a clean, washed feeling about it.

Sun—warm on my shoulders, gleaming on Renegade's shiny black coat, soaking into the saddle that smells of leather and saddle soap.

Renegade stood perfectly while I saddled him. He is waiting now, his ears pricked forward, alert but calm. I haven't taught him about the bridle and bit yet, so I slip a halter with a lead rope attached to it over his head.

I look at Marion and she smiles at me. "Swallow your nerves," she says. "You've prepared well for this moment. Enjoy it."

She leaves the round pen and stands outside, watching through the rails.

I put my foot in the stirrup. Marion has told me to mount Renegade as if I've mounted him a hundred times before. So I do, swinging my leg over his back without hesitating. I settle myself into the saddle. I let my breath out slowly.

I'm not sure I want to be here. I glance back at Marion and my heart skips a beat. She is not alone. Dad is standing beside her.

At that moment my world changes.

Dad gives me a little nod. I want to be cool but I can't help it. My face splits into an enormous grin.

I nudge Renegade with my legs, feathery touches, and he starts to walk. I hold on to the rope but I don't need to do anything. After all, there is nowhere Renegade can really go in the round pen except around and around. I sit still. Marion says that on your first ride you are a guest in your horse's house. I try to be respectful.

It is four years since I have been on a horse, but it feels like yesterday. I imagine I hear Mom's voice. *Way to go, Thea.*

Suddenly Max and Bob erupt out of nowhere, sprinting across the corral, barking their joy at finding us. It frightens Renegade, and he breaks into a trot. My heart jumps into my throat, and I'm not sure what's going to happen next. Then I hear Dad saying calmly, "Just go with it, Thea. Sit still. Breathe."

I breathe. I let my back absorb the motion. It's coming back to me now. But it helps so much that Dad is here.

My shoulders relax. Renegade and I move together as one. He trots twice around the pen and then he settles back to a walk. I lean forward and stroke his neck. His ears swivel back toward me.

I want to ride forever. I never want to get off. But Dad says that Renegade has probably had enough for his first time.

I tell Renegade *whoa* and he stands still. I slide onto the ground. Dad comes into the round pen. He strokes Renegade's neck, rubs him between his eyes.

"You've got a good horse, Thea," says Dad.

I think I will burst with pride.

Twenty-Four

Marion leaves in the afternoon. She shakes hands with Dad and Tully and Van, but she gives me a long hard hug. "Thank you," she says. "For helping me find Livia."

I ask her if she'll come back next year and she says maybe, but I don't think she will. I think Marion has finally closed this chapter of her life.

Van and I go for a walk, and I tell him two stories about my mother.

I tell him how my mother left my father and me for another man. I tell him everything, about finding out from Samantha Higgens and how I never saw my mom again.

Van listens carefully. Then he says, "She left your *father*. Not you. I bet she wouldn't have given you up. She'd have come back for you. You'd probably have ended up living with her part of the time and your dad part of the time. That's usually the way it goes."

Trust Van to think of something like that. He sounds so certain that it takes my breath away.

"Have you ever told your dad that you know?" asks Van.

"No," I say.

"Will you?"

I think about that for a moment. "I don't know. Maybe one day."

Then I tell Van the second story about my mother. That she loved me enough to give me a gift—a passion for horses. It's the best gift she could have given me. Van says he can just picture me at four years old, jogging around on a pony on the end of a rope.

My thoughts about my mother are still mixed up. Maybe they always will be. I wish more than anything that she was still alive. But I know one thing. It's not going to hurt so much to let myself remember.

Twenty-Five

At the end of the summer, a letter arrives for me. It's in a pale blue envelope and there are English stamps on it.

Dear Thea,

I thought you would like to know that Esta died this morning. She lived several weeks longer than was expected. She was comfortable at the end and didn't suffer. Our past few weeks together were very special. We talked and talked. There was so much Esta needed to let go of, and I think it gave her some relief to talk about what happened.

It may be hard for you to understand how I can forgive Esta, but she was my sister. She was fourteen when it happened, a troubled girl and terribly unhappy. I never believed that she meant to kill Livia or even meant her much harm. One foolish impulsive action, a rock thrown without thinking of the consequences, caused so much pain for so many people.

Esta answered the questions I have wondered about. Livia stopped breathing almost instantly, she said. When Esta realized that Livia was dead, she told me to go back to the cabin and say that Livia had gone with me. I was to tell no one where we had been. She said we would all get into terrible trouble if I did.

Why didn't I tell anyone that Livia had died? The truth is, I didn't know.

When Esta came back to our cabin, she told me that Livia had been pretending, that she was only frightened by the wasps. Later she said she had seen Livia with Heb. And I believed her. Or wanted to believe.

I am not a religious person but I have prayed for both Livia and Esta.

I think often of you and Renegade.

> *Your friend,*
> *Iris*

⸎

Chloe and I ride side by side, across the field and onto a trail that disappears into the sun-dappled forest. I'm riding Renegade and Chloe is on a big bay called Sam. Renegade feels powerful, like he wants to run, but he is responsive to my aids. Together, Dad and I have taught him to give softly to the bit, and he mouths it gently now. I pat his neck and tell him, "Good boy."

Chloe and I have been chattering since we left the barn. I have so much to tell her. My biggest news is that WE ARE STAYING! Last week, Tully offered Dad a job as the manager of his future stable and horse-breeding business. Tully confessed that a few days before he came into the café that night in June, he had run into one of Dad's old friends, Matt Booker, at a horse auction. Matt had told him that Dad was living in town and looking for work. "He's your man for horses," Matt had said.

"So I had my eye on you for this all along," Tully had said to Dad with a wink. "I figured you'd get tired of banging nails."

We toasted Dad's new job with champagne (a very small glass for me). Dad and Tully are out right now looking at a string of riding horses that a dude ranch in the area is selling. I love the thought of the barn being filled with horses again. I like to think that Renegade had a lot to do with this.

"What did Van say when you told him?" says Chloe. She turns and scrutinizes my face with a wicked gleam in her eyes.

My cheeks feel hot. Lately, I've been finding myself thinking a lot about the way it felt when Van held my hand when we found Livia.

I squeeze my legs against Renegade's sides and he breaks into a trot, pulling ahead of Sam and Chloe.

"Hey!" yells Chloe. For a few minutes we fly along the trail. I can hear Sam's hooves thudding behind me. We come out into an open meadow and gallop, side by side, the wind blowing in our faces.

Laughing, we pull the horses to a walk. "That was great," says Chloe.

It's a hot day and we let the horses amble home. We talk about our plans for tonight. Some of the youth-group kids are meeting in town for dinner and a movie. I'm going with Van, and Chloe is going with Mike, who she insists is just a friend.

Renegade nickers when he sees the ranch spread out below us. I stroke his neck. I know just how he feels. We're home.

Acknowledgments

I would like to thank my editor, Sarah Harvey, who always gets what I am trying to say and makes it better. I would also like to thank my sister Janet, who is never too tired to read my manuscript one more time, and my husband, Larry, who makes it possible for me to have the time to write.

Becky Citra is the author of many books for children, including *After the Fire, Never To Be Told* and *Whiteout*. Becky lives on a ranch in Bridge Lake, British Columbia, where she has ridden and trained horses for thirty years.